# The Alabaster Box

# Brittany Basham

# The Alabaster Box

# Acknowledgments

*I'd like to thank my family and God for inspiring this story. This story is written in honor of my grandmother, Jo Lawson, who raved so much over my first book, and encouraged me to write another. I'd also like to thank my mother for editing this story and always encouraging my love for writing. And my dear friend Rebecca – may you be encouraged by this tale and realize God is still penning your love story, and it's going to be grander than anything beyond your wildest dreams.*

## Author's Note

*When I sat down in September of 2017 and wrote the first chapter of this story, I was unaware it would take me an entire year to finish it. I've written much longer stories, which took me less amount of time. When God gave me the vision for this story, I was going through a dark time in my life. I've cried and laughed through the writing process, and millions of people may never read this book, but you've chosen to pick it up, and I pray it blesses you immensely. Each character name in this book was carefully chosen. They each represent a special meaning, and during biblical times, most people chose their child's name carefully, and I've done the same.*

## ***Character Names and Meanings***

*Tilly: Strength in battle.*

*Tobias: The goodness of God.*

*Caleb: Faithful*

*Trina: Pure*

*Nadine: Hope*

*Theresa: Harvester*

*Beau: Handsome*

*Thomas: Twin*

*Bart: Son of the Earth*

*Diana: Heavenly and divine*

*Rosalie: Rose*

**Chapter One**

"Mama, I still don't understand why we can't keep these cookies for ourselves!" Tilly groaned in frustration as she watched her mother press heart shaped impressions with a cookie cutter throughout the dough.

"Because these are for the church social, Tilly Ann. Don't you worry, I'll make us another batch sometime soon," her mother grinned, handing her the spoon to lick. "Shh, don't tell Nadine or Theresa," she winked as Tilly grasped the batter soaked spoon in her hand. They shared a secretive smile as Tilly licked off the gooey substance. Mother placed the cookies in the oven to bake.

"We should take a break," Mother remarked, dusting her floured hands on her apron.

"What kind of break? Could we make lemonade?" Tilly queried.

"Later, but that wasn't the kind of break I was talking about. Daniel prayed three times daily, and when I'm able, I like to stop what I'm doing and talk to the good Lord above. Paul said to pray without ceasing, and I talk to Jesus whenever I get a minute. If I truly want to reverence him, then I like to shut my bedroom door and get down on my knees and spend some time in prayer," she explained.

"Could I pray with you, Mama?" Tilly inquired, her azure irises sparkling with earnest.

"Of course, my child," Mother consented, placing her hand on the small of her back, leading her to her chamber. She and her siblings were never allowed in their parents' bedroom, so she felt extremely important to have been granted an invitation, like she'd been initiated into a secret club.

"So, what are we going to do first?" Tilly asked after her mother had closed the door.

"Well, I have something I'd like to show you," Mother said, padding to the closet. A few seconds later, she reemerged holding a white stone box.

"What's that, Mama?" Tilly queried, wrinkling her nose curiously.

"This is my alabaster box, Tilly-Ann, it holds something most precious to me," she disclosed, placing it gingerly on the bed. Tilly observed the duvet cradling the box, as if it were being held by the precious hands of Jesus himself. For a moment, she imagined it was a sacred relic instead of a family heirloom.

"What's in it?" Tilly quizzed.

"Whenever I hear there's a need in the church or from one of our neighbors, I take a small piece of paper and I write down a prayer request. I fold up the paper and slip it into the box, and I pray over it daily," she expounded.

"Does Daddy know about your box?" Tilly inquired.

"No, it's a private matter. This box belonged to my grandmother, and she passed it on to me; she's the one that taught me how to pray. Your daddy doesn't know about it because there are requests in here about him," she chortled.

Tilly nodded in understanding. "What about me, Mama? Are there any prayers in there about me?"

"Yes, my dear, there are prayers in here about you and your siblings," Mother illuminated.

"What are some of the things you've been praying about concerning me?" Tilly inquired with piqued interest.

Mother smiled thoughtfully. "That you'll grow up to become a beautiful God-fearing woman." She kissed her russet curls affectionately, dismounting onto her knees. "Now will you pray with me, Tilly?"

"Yes, Mama," she replied, dropping onto her knees beside her mother, and folding her hands. She closed her eyes, peeping every once and awhile to find her mother weeping and clenching the alabaster box as she poured out prayers of thanksgiving and supplication to God. Tilly did her best to pray like Mama, and her mother had told her that God hears our prayers and they didn't need to sound eloquent. She didn't pray as long as Mama, and she couldn't remember everything she talked to God about, however she did remember asking God to transform her into a fervent prayer warrior like her mother. To have an unwavering faith like her mother, would be an answered prayer indeed.

## Chapter Two

Tilly Ann tapped her pencil against her temple, contemplating on what she should write next. Tomorrow she would deliver her book report to her entire seventh grade class. This shouldn't have been a difficult assignment for her, but she found herself struggling to find the proper words. She worried her lower lip with her slightly crooked row of bottom teeth. She placed her pencil on the parchment, ready to write the first sentence when she heard a loud bang resound from the kitchen. Tilly abandoned her task, hurrying to the kitchen to find her mother laying prostrate on the floor.

"Mama!" she cried, shaking her hard. The tea kettle on the stove whistled. In a few swift seconds she felt her pa pulling her off of her mother.

"Go get Doc Jacobs!" he commanded.

Tilly ran out of the house, her skirts swishing as she sprinted down the dirt lane to fetch the doctor which lived only a few houses down from their farm. Her lungs pleaded for oxygen as she ran up the steps, pounding furiously on the door.

"Doc Jacobs! it's Tilly! Ma has fallen and she's hurt!" she bellowed.

A middle-aged woman, with auburn hair styled in a messy bun greeted her at the door. "Matilda Matthews, what on earth is wrong!?" Mrs. Jacobs demanded.

"My Ma collapsed, Mrs. Jacobs. Pa sent me to retrieve Doc Jacobs," she respired, her breath coming out in uneven gasps.

"Hold on, darlin'! I'll go get him!" she responded, rushing hastily from the door.

Tilly wasn't sure if hours or minutes had passed when Doc Jacobs finally made it to the door. He and his wife piled into their old town car, sandwiching her between them as they made their way back to the Matthews' residence. When they burst through the door, Tilly immediately knew something was amiss, as her father, three elder brothers, and two younger sisters crowded around their mother, tears streaming down their faces.

"May I have a look?" Dr. Jacobs inquired gently, glancing at Bart Matthews ruefully.

He granted him a solemn nod, moving aside so that he

could assess Diana Matthews. Doc Jacobs bent down beside the unconscious woman, placing two fingers against her pulse point. He gazed up at Bart, shaking his head sorrowfully as he rose to his feet. An anguished cry could be heard throughout the Matthews' residence as the doctor's silent gesture registered within their minds. Rosalie Jacobs pulled the younger girls to her side as Bart wept like a baby over his deceased wife. The boys gathered around their father and did the same. Tilly Ann felt tears cascade down her cheeks, the image of her mother's lifeless body lying on the floor burned into her subconscious forever. Diana Matthews was pronounced dead at the age of 37, after suffering cardiac arrest.

On the day of her mother's funeral, the preacher at their small country church spoke words from the scriptures which Tilly had never fully taken the time to understand, old sayings about love and Heaven where her mother was now. However Tilly wasn't concerned about God or anything her mother had taught her to believe anymore. God had cruelly stolen their mother away from them, and she couldn't find it in her heart to care about faith or Sunday school when she was trying to wrap her fragile mind around something she would never be able to truly comprehend. They shoveled dirt over her mother's grave, leaving everything she'd ever been taught to believe in shambles. Nothing made sense, and Tilly wasn't sure if it ever would again. At the fledgling age of 12, Tilly Matthews became the woman of the house, and she resented it every day.

Tilly's world wasn't the only one which fell apart, though. Bart Matthews started drinking, and the family quit going to Sunday meeting. Their mama had been the heart of their God-fearing family, and without her their faith had collapsed. No more hymns were sung around the dinner table, and no more bedtime prayers were said. The Matthews put away all their 'God nonsense', as their daddy called it and resumed their lives without it, but nothing was ever the same, and their circumstances didn't improve because without the guidance of Christ, their family became like a scattered flock.

## Chapter Three

Tilly Ann tugged at her bonnet, wrapping her shawl tightly around her shoulders as she gazed at her mother's tombstone. She exhaled sharply, her chilled breath appearing in wisps in front of her. It had started to snow, but no matter how numb she felt on the outside – it couldn't compare with how frigid she was feeling within. An icy glaze had formed around her heart and nothing could seem to thaw it.

"Mama, I'm trying to make sure the girls have a decent Christmas. Beau and Thomas shot a buck, so we'll be cooking deer stew for Christmas dinner. Pa says the crops haven't been worth a flip this year. I think it's 'cause he drinks all the time and doesn't spend enough time in the fields. Nothing has been the same since you left us. Doc Jacobs and Mrs. Jacobs sent toys for the girls. I reckon they're both getting dolls. At least that's what I heard. I didn't ask for anything, but Mrs. Jacobs bought me an art set. She told me I should paint more, that it'll help stabilize my emotions. No amount of painting is going to heal my heart though. She doesn't realize when you left, a great cavern formed. It'll never be filled, Mama. I'm trying to do right by the girls because they're too little to understand, but some days I feel like I just can't go on," she whimpered, wiping at her eyes.

A brisk wind tousled her curls, and she knew her nose was turning red. Neither her Pa nor her siblings knew she'd sneaked out of the house to visit her mother's grave. No one wanted to talk about it anymore, but Tilly refused to make her a distant memory. It was Christmas Day, and they'd usually be in the kitchen all day baking sweets. She recounted the gingerbread men and the funny faces she'd decorated with icing. Her mother always baked them for the children in their Sunday school class, but the ones which didn't turn out right ended up in their own cookie jar. Tilly hated to admit she purposefully messed up several of the faces, so they'd be able to keep more of the cookies for themselves. She beamed at the memory; it warmed her heart as she recounted her mother's infectious laughter and radiant smile. She gazed up at the gray expanse. A snowflake fell from the heavens, landing on the bridge of her nose. She brushed it away, diverting her attention back to the headstone. She kissed her gloved hand, placing it gently on the edge of the stone.

"Merry Christmas, Mama," she added, turning away to head home.

She was startled when she saw Reverend Vann standing a few feet away, cane poised in front of him.

"Reverend." Tilly nodded respectfully at the older man.

"Miss Matthews, you should get home before the storm hits. It's no day for a young lady like yourself to be frolicking about. It's Christmas after all," he stated.

Tilly shrugged her shoulders. "I came to see my Ma, Reverend. Surely you can understand that."

"I can, and I do. Cynthia has been gone for ten years; I actually stopped by to place fresh flowers on her grave. Poinsettias were her favorite, and I purchase several from the florist each year and bring them by." He offered her a sympathetic smile, melancholy briefly flickering across his gaze.

"I'm sorry about your wife, Reverend. I hope you'll have a Merry Christmas," she replied sympathetically.

"Tilly, I haven't seen you or your family at any of the services in awhile. Is everything alright?" he pried.

Tilly stiffened at his inquiry but didn't bother turning

around. “We're fine, Reverend. It’s just, taking care of youngins' ain't easy. The girls are difficult to corral during the mornings, and Mama isn't around to keep 'em in line. Pa is doing the best he can, manning the fields, and we just don't have the time,” she answered, refusing to dispel the truth. The boys never cared much for church, though they were compliant to attend whenever their mother made them. She was the glue which had held their faith and family together, and without her they were unraveling at the seams. Tilly didn't know what to do nor did she understand. The God her mother had spoken so fondly of seemed so distant and unreachable. The last day she'd spent with her, they'd closed the door to her bedroom and prayed. It felt like such a faraway memory now. Tilly had often tried to copy the words her mother had spoken in prayer, but they always fell flat. She'd adored her mother, but she had to face the facts and realize the God her mother devotedly served didn't care about her. He'd taken her mother away, and she didn't desire to know him, no matter how many Bible stories she recounted about his unfailing love and faithfulness. He wasn't for her.

It began to snow, steadily blanketing the countryside. Reverend Vann had shouted something behind her, but the wind muffled his declaration and she didn't hear him. She didn't bother turning around to continue their conversation as she walked back to a house which was no longer a home.

Reverend Vann smiled somberly, gingerly plucking one of the poinsettias from the bouquet of flowers he'd brought for his wife. He placed in on Diana Matthew's grave. “Merry Christmas, Diana, I'm praying your family has their faith renewed. You were truly one of a kind, and I pray those children remember your example.”

The reverend limped away, back towards his parsonage, temporarily forgetting the prayer he'd recently prayed, but God had heard him, and an answer he would supply.

## Chapter Four

The sun beamed down heavily upon the farm; it was a sweltering day. Tilly scattered chicken feed across the ground, her comrade, Trina, trailing close behind.

"No offense, Tilly, but I don't understand why you won't attend this Sunday's social with me! It's the first one of the new year. They're having dinner on the ground, Lewis and his band are going to play some old gospel hymns, and we might go swimmin' in the creek, if it's warm enough," Trina appealed. The redhead rocked back and forth on her heels, her hands swinging at her sides.

Tilly glanced back at Trina. "You know why I can't go. I have responsibilities to attend to, and it's my job to keep Nadine and Theresa in line. They count on me. Pa relies on me to make sure the house is clean and our meals are on the table."

Trina exhaled sharply. "Bring 'em with you! You need to get out of this place before you smother yourself to death with household duties."

Tilly chuckled humorlessly, perching a hand on her petite hip. “Do you really believe it's that easy? I wish I could take a day off, go back to school with the rest of my classmates, attend Sunday socials, swim in the creek, and stuff myself silly with homemade ice cream. Chores don't go away and little girls need guidance. Ma is out of the picture, and I had no choice but to step up to the plate.”

Trina held up her hands defensively. “I'm sorry for being so brash. It's just, you're my friend, and I don't want you to miss out on life. There's so much we've yet to experience. Your Ma always took your family to church. Why'd you stop going?” She touched Tilly's shoulder softly, awaiting a response.

Tilly cringed at the mention of church. She'd answered Trina's exact question, many ways to different people. “We don't go anymore, that's all there is to it,” she remarked gruffly.

Trina decided not to press the matter further, quelling her tongue instead. “Alright, well I better be heading back home. Mother wants to go visit Charlotte Trenton. Her daughter just arrived home from England. Apparently she's been attending some fancy boarding school in London.”

“Must be nice to be born with a silver spoon in your mouth,” Tilly spat out bitterly.

Trina shrugged. “I suppose, her name's Julia, and mother believes we'll have common interests since we're the same age. Mother simply longs to fit into aristocratic society. Mrs. Trenton knows we're dirt poor; I think she's just trying to be hospitable.”

“It's amazing the lengths people will go to impress others,” Tilly scoffed, picking up an empty milk bucket.

“Come on, there's got to be at least one person you've tried to impress,” Trina insisted.

Tilly licked her chapped lips, gifting Trina with a wistful smile. “There was someone, but she's gone.” She barely whispered, traipsing in the other direction. Tears stung at her eyes, she quickly wiped them away as her mother's face emerged in her mind. It had nearly been a year since her passing, but the pain was still fresh – a festering wound which wouldn't heal. She hid behind her pain, it was what kept her going – made her stronger. It was all she had left to hold on to as she forced herself day after day to fulfill the monotonous routines farm life demanded. She thrust the milk bucket against the barn and it resounded with a loud clang. She plucked it off the ground and threw it again and again, until hot tears blurred her vision. She'd shed too many tears, and when she'd imagined she didn't have any left, she'd find there was still more left to cry.

"You're gonna dent that bucket if you don't stop that nonsense," a deep masculine voice resounded from behind. Tilly's blood chilled in her veins as she turned around to meet her father's calculating glance.

Tilly swallowed hard. "I'm sorry, Pa, I just got angry." Her voice carried a nervous tinge, and she loathed how weak she sounded.

"Come 'ere, pumpkin." The brawny man held his arms open for her, and without a second thought, she lunged into his arms. He pulled her into his secure embrace, patting her back with his rough hands, consolingly. She inhaled his musky scent of sweat and earth, but there was a hint of something else – a swirling iridescent liquid he savored during his spare time. Her heart plummeted in her chest when she realized her daddy had been drinking. He wasn't usually this affectionate, but the shine loosened him up. She inhaled sharply, knowing it was fruitless to ask him about the Sunday social when he was sober. Work came first, and the duties of farm life were unending. She felt guilty taking advantage of him, but her heart craved freedom.

Tilly broke the hug, glancing into her father's glassy eyes.

"Pa, do you think I could attend the Sunday social with Trina this weekend? I promise to wake up extra early to complete my chores if you say yes," she asked hopefully.

"Sure thing, pumpkin. I reckon you're a hard worker, smart as a tack, too. Caleb can watch your sisters while you're gone, but I expect you home by five to help with the milking," he consented.

Tilly's face brightened with mirth. She stood on her tiptoes, pressing a kiss against his sun kissed jaw. "Thank you so much, Pa!" Tilly grabbed the discarded bucket, flouncing away. A hearty grin stretched across her face; she surmised her face would crack from smiling so much, but this was the most exuberant she'd been in months. She was certain a reunion with her classmates would help remedy her dour mood and make her feel like a kid again.

## Chapter Five

Tilly whizzed through her chores, her mind circulating around Sunday. She hummed a catchy tune, dancing barefoot through the kitchen as she swept the floor.

"Why are you in such a chipper mood for?"

She halted the broom, glancing up to see her brother, Caleb, perched against the egress, chomping on a gala apple. He stood nearly six feet tall, curly blond hair falling in his face. He was two years older than her, already fifteen, but still the younger of her two other brothers.

Tilly steadied her gaze on him; a cunning smile gracing her lips when she recounted her father telling her he could watch their baby sisters while she attended the social.

"You got a staring problem now? Want me to wipe that smirk off your face?" he threatened emptily, tossing his apple core at her feet. It rolled across the floor, and she scowled at him. She poised the broom above her head, the sudden urge to whack him with it crossing her mind. She thought better of it, knowing she needed to be on her best behavior if she wished to attend the social.

Caleb stepped back, raising his hands up in surrender as she aimed the broom for his head. He clenched his eyes shut, awaiting the blow. Instead, he heard obnoxious peals of laughter. "You should have seen your face!" Tilly stuck her index finger out, guffawing.

Caleb rolled his eyes, crossing his arms loosely under his chest. "Ha Ha, you got me," he remarked acerbically.

Tilly smirked at her brother, positioning the broom in front of her. "If you must know, Pa told me I could go to the Sunday social tomorrow."

"Okay, and who's going to watch the girls?" he asked, his face dawning with realization. "Wait a second, oh no, not happening!"

Tilly's countenance fell. "Please, Caleb, I never get to go anywhere. I need this, some time to myself so I don't go berserk!" she lamented, pulling at the ends of her chestnut ringlets.

A sly smile tugged at the teen's lips. He tapped his chin in contemplation. "Hold on a minute...is my sister actually begging me for a favor?"

Tilly groaned at his theatrics. “Cough it up, I know there's something you want,” she deadpanned.

Caleb placed his hands behind his head, tiptoeing around a mound of dirt she'd gathered with the broom. “Well, there is one thing. I want you to ask Trina if she likes me,” he blurted out.

Tilly coughed, nearly choking on her saliva. “Excuse me? What did you say?”

Caleb allowed his arms to fall to his sides, his expression becoming pensive. “I really like her, okay? Just ask her what she thinks of me, without dispelling the truth about my affections,” he mumbled, his cheeks blooming with heat.

Tilly nodded. “Fine, I'll ask her.”

Caleb's features softened. “Good, now what do I need to do about the girls?”

Tilly took the time to explain their sisters' daily routines, from feeding times to naps. Caleb had settled on making everyone ham sandwiches with sliced fruit for lunch since Tilly would be absent. None of the men in her family could really cook unless it was wild game. She made a mental note to teach Caleb a few simple recipes he could make if she decided to venture out again. Who was she kidding? This was a one time opportunity.

She'd be fortunate if she was allowed to attend Trina's birthday in the late summer. Thirteen was an important age, though Tilly hadn't done anything special for her own celebration – still a girl- not quite yet a woman. There were issues she was facing she wished her mother were here to school her about. She recounted the morning she'd awoken with blood-stained linens. Worried she was dying, she'd stormed to the Jacobs' residence, only to discover her menstrual cycle had arrived. Mrs. Jacobs had consoled her, gifted her with some linen scraps to keep clean, smiled proudly at her and announced she was a woman. She supposed she was a woman, for she had stepped into her mother's shoes the moment she'd passed.

Tilly pushed those bleak thoughts from her mind, opting to focus on what she could bring to the Sunday social. She'd settled on making her mother's famous chocolate oatmeal cookies – simple and easy. It was mid-May, and it was a sticky and humid day. She'd donned her sky blue cotton dress, her russet curls falling down her back in silken waves. Her luscious flowing locks had been the envy of the other girls in her class. She traipsed down the lane, the plate of cookies balanced precariously in her arms. The church was just a five minute walk from their farm. The churchyard was bustling with activity when she arrived. There were tables covered in white linen cloths, arrayed with dishes of various food.

Lewis Gribble's bluegrass band played in the background, thrumming tunes to familiar hymns which caused a wave of despondency to overshadow her. She swallowed down her grief as images of her mother singing in their country church filled her subconscious. Her gaze darted around, searching for a distraction. She heaved a sigh of relief when she spied, Trina, seated on a checkered picnic blanket. She deposited her cookies on the dessert table and made a beeline for her comrade.

Trina was giggling with another girl she vaguely recognized. The other girl had stunning sapphire eyes, and Shirley Temple blonde curls, which framed her delicate, heart-shaped face.

"Trina!" Tilly grinned, arresting the redhead's attention.

Trina peered up to see the brunette standing in front of her. "Oh my goodness, you scared me, Tilly! I wasn't expecting you to be here," she remarked, startled.

"I'm sorry to barge in, but it was a truly last minute decision. Caleb agreed to watch Nadine and Theresa for a few hours, so Pa said I could come." Tilly shrugged, rubbing her arms to generate warmth. She noticed the blonde haired girl was glowering, scrutinizing her appearance from head to toe, as if she'd crawled from a rubbish bin. Tilly's stomach flip-flopped uncomfortably.

"It's alright!" Trina smiled warmly. "By the way, Tilly, this is Julia Trenton. Julia, meet Tilly Matthews."

"A pleasure," Julia remarked curtly.

"Nice to meet you, too," Tilly stammered, seating herself beside Trina – the only safe barrier between her and Julia.

"Are you hungry, Tilly? Want me to get you a plate?" Trina offered.

"Nah I'm fine, really," Tilly insisted, granting her a modest smile.

"Well if you're not getting her anything, could you perhaps procure me some more punch?" Julia proposed in her sweet syrupy voice. She waved the glass back and forth in front of Trina's face.

"Sure," Trina replied politely, taking the cup from her grasp and flouncing away.

"So, you live on a farm, Trina tells me." Julia granted her an assessing glance. Tilly felt her chest swarm with angry bees.

She was trying her hardest to ignore Julia, so why did she insist on being chatty?

"Um, yeah." Tilly shrugged, schooling her features so she didn't pick up on her discomfort. She had an inkling Julia enjoyed making people feel intimidated. Tilly immediately saw through her 'charming' rich girl facade. She'd been staring daggers at her since the moment she'd arrived.

"Is that what they wear on the farm nowadays, those things?" Julia inquired, gesticulating to her plain cotton dress – one her mother had sewn with so much love and fondness. Tears sprung to her eyes as a memory assaulted her cognition – the one where her mother had taught her how to sew.

"My mother made it," she mumbled quietly, feeling her insecurities rear their ugly head.

Julia scoffed loudly. "Was she blind because the stitching is off."

Tilly whipped her head around, her eyes filled with pure vexation as this blonde dolt insulted her mother's handiwork. Blind, hot rage consumed her; she lunged at Julia, knocking her to the ground. Julia squealed, calling for help as Tilly drew her fist back, ready to strike. She never had the chance because she felt two lithe arms wrapping around her like vise grips, hauling her away from Julia Trenton.

"Your Mama would have switched your behind if she ever caught you fightin', Tilly-Ann!" Rosalie Jacobs admonished, gifting the teen with a stern look.

Tilly glanced around warily; they were out of earshot of most people. "She insulted my dress, and I usually wouldn't have reacted that way, but Mama made it for me! It's the only one I have left that still fits." Tilly sniffled, feeling like a lost and forlorn little girl.

Rosalie exhaled sharply, cupping Tilly's face in her weathered hands. "You've got to be strong, darlin'. I know it's hard. I lost my mother when I was around your age, too, but God must have a plan for all of this. It ain't fair, and I'm not sure I quite understand it myself, but you must make peace with it. Your mama wouldn't want you bottling up all that animosity in your heart over her loss. You got to let it go; she's up there singing with the angels, and she wants you to find your song again, too."

"Maybe, but how? I'm 13, and I've become a mother. I can barely coerce myself out of bed some days. Pa, my brothers, and the girls all depend on me, but I can't do it. I don't have the strength! I feel so lost and alone," she sniffled.

Rosalie kissed her fevered brow, pulling her in for a tight hug. "But you're not alone, Tilly. I'm here, and I'll do whatever it takes to help you through this, and so will the good Lord. You're so much stronger than you think, my dear."

Tilly shook her head, pulling away from the middle-aged woman. "I'm not strong, I'm weak and inadequate," she berated herself.

Rosalie chuckled. "You know, there was a man named, Gideon, who felt the same way you do."

Tilly blinked owlishly. "Gideon? Please enlighten me."

Rosalie encouraged Tilly to sit under a nearby maple tree with her. She pulled out her Bible and read from Judges chapter 6, about a man named, Gideon. She told her how he and his meager army of 300 soldiers devastated a Midianite camp, after God told him he'd already secured the victory for him. She discovered Gideon felt weak and unqualified, but God saw him as a mighty warrior. Rosalie stressed the point of the story was that without God, Gideon's victory would have been impossible.

"Mama always said nothing is impossible with God," Tilly added after Mrs. Jacobs had closed her Bible.

"Precisely, Tilly, and that's why you need to hold on to

those truths your mother has instilled in you, and teach them to your sisters. They need you to be an example to them, to guide them along the path of righteousness. Your Daddy isn't going to take a stand, but you can. Your Mama sure instilled a lot of trust in you," Rosalie commended.

Rosalie's comment hit her like a ton of bricks. Her mind gravitated back to the final day she'd spent with her mother, locked in her prayer room. Tears streamed down her face in realization – the alabaster box.

"Mama told me her prayer was for me to turn into a God-fearing woman," she confided in the doctor's wife.

"Then become that woman, Tilly. In this life, we'll face many hardships, but Hebrews 13:5 says, he'll never leave us or forsake us. He'll stick closer to you than a brother. I know you don't see it now, but one day you'll see he's all you've ever needed. He'll be faithful to you, just watch and see," Rosalie encouraged her.

Rosalie's words resonated in her mind throughout the remainder of the day and into the night. She mulled over them, and pondered upon them excessively. Had the cruel God she'd conjured in her mind existed at all? Had she been mistaken this whole time? The God her mother proclaimed was merciful and forgiving - a righteousness judge. As she attempted to piece together this vital revelation, and put things into proper perspective, she found herself drifting off to sleep. A warm presence reminiscent of sunshine coursed through her while she slept – one her mother had so often described as being the hand of almighty God.

## Chapter Six

Tilly had left the social without any incident. Rosalie Jacobs had driven her home, promising not to breathe a word of it to her father as long as it didn't happen again. Caleb had been waiting for her at the door, like an old barn cat begging for some scraps.

“So, what did she say?” he'd inquired discreetly.

Tilly shook her head. “I'll talk to you about it in the morning; I'm not feeling so good.” She'd heard Caleb mutter something obscenely under his breath as she'd sought out the sanctuary of her room. She'd practically collapsed on the bed, utterly spent from the events of the day. She'd hazily opened her eyes the following morning, readied herself, and began her daily chores. A quarter till 10, a candy apple red 1954 BMW Roadster pulled up to the farm. It looked like it'd just been driven off Mr. Vicksburg's car lot. A woman wearing a canary yellow afternoon dress stepped from the vehicle. She had a black pocketbook under her arm, and a large floppy sunhat covered her head. Her black suede pumps stirred the dust as she walked down the driveway. Tilly immediately stopped what she was doing, heading over to greet the stranger.

"May I help you, mam?" The young girl asked, feeling under dressed when she caught a glimpse of the woman's immaculate apparel.

The woman smiled friendlily at her, flashing her gleaming white teeth. "Yes, I'm Charlotte Trenton, and I was looking for a Mr. Matthews."

Tilly gulped back the bile forming in her throat. *'Oh no,'* she thought. She was surely in for it now. "My Pa is out in the fields, I can go fetch him for you," she offered, unable to hide the nervous edge to her voice.

Charlotte blinked in realization, removing her sunhat – her dark blonde curls glittering gold in the sunlight. "You're the girl who tried to punch my Julia!" She stuck out her index finger accusingly.

"Yes, Mam, and I'm real sorry about that. Julia hurt my feelings; she made fun of my dress. It was one my mother sewed for me shortly before she passed," Tilly dispelled.

Charlotte's gaze softened. "My condolences, Tilly. I'll handle Julia once I arrive home, but you still shouldn't be fighting. It's uncouth and unladylike," she chided.

"Yes, and my mama raised me better, I just let my temper get the best of me," she sighed exhaustively – the tension evident in her shoulders.

"What's this I hear about you starting fights, young lady!?" Her daddy's voice boomed in the background.

Tilly clenched her eyes shut, unable to meet his gaze. Luckily, Charlotte Trenton, decided to rescue her. "Your daughter and mine had a teeny squabble. It's nothing to fret over. The matter has been resolved. I'm Charlotte Trenton by the way, and you are?" She held out an elegant gloved hand for her father to shake. Bart Matthews nearly dropped the buckwheat thistle hanging from his mouth. He wiped his greasy hands on his denim overalls, reaching out to give her hand a firm shake.

"I'm Bart Matthews, Mam, and this here's my farm," he remarked, star struck.

"It's a quaint little place you have here," she chortled musically.

"Yeah, um, would you like a tour?" he offered.

"I'd love one!" she exclaimed, looping her arm through the farmer's as – like they were old friends – he escorted her around their property.

Tilly blinked owlishly, not fully comprehending what had just transpired. It was no secret, Charlotte Trenton's husband was the president and C.E.O. Of an international banking corporation. He was rarely ever home, and when Julia went back to boarding school that following fall, her mother began spending more time around the farm. It was almost comical to watch the ritzy woman milk cows and gather eggs. She was very much out of her element, Tilly thought.

One afternoon when she'd finished milking the cows, she spied Caleb perched against the barn. “Why ain't you working?” Tilly implored, transfixing her gaze on her idle brother.

“Tilly, don't you realize what's going on here?” Caleb gave her a wary look.

“What do you mean?” she quizzed.

“Beau and Thomas both know it, so I might as well tell you. You're old enough to understand. Pa and Mrs. Trenton ain't spending time together just 'cause he's teaching her about the farm. They're having an affair,” he dispelled in a harsh whisper.

Tilly's head began to spin, her young mind conjuring up the word “adultery” and how her mama always taught her that breaking a marriage covenant was a terrible sin. It tore families apart and shattered lives.

"But why would he!?" she reasoned, unable to form a practical response.

Caleb chuckled humorlessly. "And why wouldn't he? Ma is gone. Mrs. Trenton's daughter nor husband are hardly ever home. It's quite the opportune time if you ask me."

The blond haired boy's features were schooled, but Tilly knew deep down he was hurting. They may not have attended church anymore, but their mother's example of righteous living still affected their hearts.

"So, what are we going to do?" Tilly appealed.

"Nothin', just keep yer mouth shut, take care of the girls and continue on like everything's okay," he forewarned.

For the first time in a long time, Tilly got down on her knees and prayed that night. She prayed God would cease what was going on with her father and Mrs. Trenton and make things right. Not even a week later, Tilly heard through the grapevine that Malcolm Trenton had been asked to move to Europe to oversee some foreign branches of his banking company, and he'd whisked his family away with him. It was a startling revelation to her father that Mrs. Trenton actually loved her millions more than him. It broke his heart, but served him right, Tilly thought. Eventually he quit his moping and buried himself in his work. The affair may have stopped, but his drinking hadn't. It kept Tilly on her toes, but she managed to get by, and life remained relatively the same for her. Nothing much changed, and Tilly decided it was probably best to stop daydreaming and become satisfied with the mundane.

## Chapter Seven

Sunsets were supposed to portray beautiful imagery and infinite hued patterns. Tilly sat outside the farm one summer evening, attempting to capture the splendor of God's canvas. She groaned inwardly, laying her brush aside. She'd earned a little money by selling one of her lambs and decided to reward herself with some new paint, an easel, and a set of blank canvases. She'd spent her free time painting scenery around the farm, but a sunset was one thing she couldn't seem to capture. Tossing her creation in the rubbish heap had crossed her mind, until a pair of childish hands grazed her backside. She instinctively turned to find, Nadine, peering over her shoulder at the painting inquisitively.

“So pretty, Sissy, paint more!” The child clapped her hands exuberantly, eliciting a smile from the eldest Matthews' daughter.

“You truly like it?” she remarked, tenderness masking her

features.

“Oh, yes! Paint more!” Nadine insisted, plopping down beside her.

Tilly began to mix oranges and reds, wondering if God saw human beings as her sister viewed her obsolete sunset – his most remarkable creation. She'd desired to toss it aside, but her sister perceived an unforeseen beauty on her splattered canvas. Did God see her like that, see her as some priceless treasure others had all but overlooked? Where had such an uncanny thought originated from? It was almost as if her mother were whispering such concepts in her ears to ponder upon. Her mother had been gone nearly four years, and she'd made up her mind to carry on – be the woman of the house and make sure her sisters' fragile existence didn't shatter. Nadine and Theresa hadn't known their mother. Tilly had been the only maternal figure in their lives. She often wondered what life would've been like for them if she were still around. She smiled bleakly at her sunset, casting a glance at Nadine.

“So, what do you think?” Tilly inquired, yearning for her younger sister's approval.

“Pretty, so pretty,” Nadine gushed, plopping a wet kiss against her cheek before flouncing away.

Tilly bit her lip uncertainly. No, she would keep the sunset. Perhaps she'd even hang it in the kitchen, so when she saw it she'd be reminded of this day – the day her sister perceived something beautiful in something so unoriginal. Tilly painted often, but she'd never imagined the sunset would quickly become her favorite. It wasn't anywhere close to being her greatest masterpiece, but the memory behind it was what made it so special. She secretly hoped someone would one day find as much beauty in her as Nadine had found in her mediocre sunset.

Tilly had reluctantly hung the painting over the stove, a reminder of the precious memory she'd made that afternoon. She'd often assess it while she cooked – the slightly smudged colors staring back at her. No matter how flawed it was, she couldn't bring herself to throw it away. Caleb had made fun of it, told her it resembled some rejected grammar school kid's fair art. Instead of being cross with him, she'd laughed at his childish remark. He'd furrowed his brow and walked away, shaking his head.

Tilly continued to paint and improve her skills. Mrs. Jacobs had stopped by one afternoon with some fresh baked cookies for Theresa's birthday. When she'd came into the house, she marveled at all of Tilly's paintings displayed on the walls.

"Matilda-Ann, did you paint all of these?" The doctor's wife inquired, awestruck.

"Yes, Mrs. Jacobs, I did. I paint as much as possible in my spare time," she replied.

A huge grin stretched across her face. "You should come with me to the city art show. Most of the galleries will be filled with professional art, but they're hosting a contest for amateurs. You should enter one of your paintings; there's a cash prize of two hundred dollars," Rosalie insisted.

"Two hundred dollars!?" The brunette gasped in consternation, nearly dropping the platter of baked chicken she'd just removed from the oven.

"Yes!" Mrs. Jacobs beamed brilliantly.

"I'll have to give it some thought," the teen mumbled, overwhelmed.

"There's another whole month before the deadline, so think it over," she returned.

"I-I-I will!" Tilly stammered, feeling hopeful and exuberant about something for the first time in months.

In the end, her father had permitted her to go to the

gallery showing. She'd decided to enter the contest, settling on a painting of the mountain view behind her back property. Mrs. Jacobs had made the entire event into a spectacle, renting an extravagant hotel room for them to stay in and buying her a chocolate mousse from a gourmet creamery – it was the best dessert she'd ever put in her mouth.

"Mrs. Jacobs, why are you doing all of this for me? You've made this day so special," Tilly inquired later that evening at the hotel.

As Mrs. Jacobs pulled the curlers from her hair, a small smile played upon her lips. "I've always wanted a daughter, and you're the closest I'll ever come to having one."

Tilly was stunned by her declaration. "Why is that, Mrs. Jacobs? There are lots of other girls more suited for formal outings such as this one. I'm merely a simple, farm girl." Her voice trailed off. She fixed her gaze on the soft pink floral wallpaper lining the walls of their hotel room – the perfect distraction to keep herself from meeting Mrs. Jacob's knowing eyes.

The older woman cupped her cheek, caressing it softly with her thumb. The motherly gesture caused tears to prickle behind Tilly's eyes. It'd been years since anyone had touched her so tenderly. She hadn't realized how much she'd been craving paternal affection until that moment. “You're so much more than you believe, beautiful girl. Our father above says you're fearfully and wonderfully made. I know you're struggling to fit into the role you've been assigned, but there's a purpose behind it. I firmly believe God has more for you in store than you can ask, think, or imagine. You're going to be surprised when you look back one day and see how he's been working behind the scenes, orchestrating your every step.” Rosalie kissed the brunette's crown of hair affectionately.

Tilly felt something deep within herself begin to break as tears spilled over her lashes. She clung to the other woman, sobbing into her nightgown. Rosalie wrapped her arms tightly around Tilly as she wept, whispering tender affirmations within her ear.

Once Tilly managed to compose herself, she glanced up at Mrs. Jacobs, wiping her nose on her own nightdress. She knew her eyes were rimmed red, and she probably looked a mess. “I'm sorry for breaking down like that,” she mumbled apologetically, her voice cracking with emotion.

Rosalie brushed her remaining tears away with her thumb. “Crying cleanses the soul. David said in Psalm 56:8, that God collects all of our tears and places them in a bottle."

Tilly blinked owlishly at her statement. "Then God must have thousands of bottles filled with my tears because one surely wouldn't suffice." A watery chuckle escaped her lips as she wiped fresh tears away. "Once I start crying I can't manage to stop."

Rosalie patted her back gently. "Cry as much as you need to, Darlin'. I'm not going to judge you for it."

Tilly felt her shoulders relax from her admission. It felt freeing to spill her heart out to someone she knew wasn't going to berate her for her fickle emotions. "Do you think I have a chance of winning the cash prize tomorrow?" she inquired sheepishly.

"You have as much of a chance as anyone else; the painting you entered is lovely. I believe it captures the true likeness of the mountain ranges and forestry surrounding your farm," she reassured her.

Rosalie's encouragement was the boost of confidence she'd needed. She'd slept fitfully that night, anticipating what the next day entailed. She'd awoken with a spring in her step – ready to take on the world. The Jacobs had gifted her with a brand new lace-trimmed Faille dress for the occasion. Mrs.

Jacobs had helped her pick it out at a local boutique back home – one she'd never been able to afford anything from herself.

The gallery showing featured more art than Tilly could swallow. There were abstract paintings, portraits of people she didn't recognize, impressionist art, and paintings with a surrealistic effect. Her mind felt as if it were going into sensory overdrive, as Mrs. Jacobs guided her to the exhibit where her painting hung.

She gazed around at the other aspiring artists which had entered pieces of their own. She kept mentally categorizing the best from the worst, surmising hers fell somewhere in between. A group of professional art critics ambled through the showroom, stopping and assessing each painting. They'd scribble down notes in their small black notebooks, make a comment or two to the artist, and move on.

Tilly felt her palms dampening with perspiration when the judges finally approached her. A woman wearing too much rouge, with silver curls framing her aged face, stared intently at her painting. Her azure irises sparkled with intrigue. "What inspired you to paint this?" she inquired, transfixing her gaze on Tilly. Tilly gazed up at the older woman, her floral perfume overpowering her senses. She felt dizzy from the intoxication but managed to steady herself enough to speak. The other judges peered at her expectantly, awaiting her answer. However they seemed to fade into the background, her eyes gravitating to the elegantly dressed woman's face.

"My mother always admired the Appalachian Mountains, and we have a grand view of them right behind our farm. One evening after I'd finished my chores, I decided I wanted to paint them. Everything my mother showed appreciation for has always inspired me. I like to keep her memory alive and painting the mountain ranges allowed me to feel close to her somehow. I imagine her view from Heaven of those mountains is far grander than mine," Tilly supplied, her hands clasped at her waist, feet poised primly together.

The older woman smiled fondly at Tilly, satisfied with her answer. "Well you certainly captured their likeness well, and I'm sure your mother would be proud," she praised, squeezing her shoulder lightly before passing on to the next contestant.

Tilly released the large gulp of air she'd unknowingly been holding, stealing a glance at Rosalie. The auburn haired woman was grinning from ear to ear. "The woman which just complimented your painting is a world renowned artist. Her name is Starla Hennessee, and she has exceptional influence in the art realm."

"So, she's truly distinguished, and it's imperative I impress her, especially if I want to win the cash prize," Tilly concluded.

Rosalie laughed heartily, pulling her in for a tight hug. "I believe you've already won her over, my dear, girl," she whispered in her ear confidently.

Tilly opted to say nothing, deciding to keep her emotions in check. She didn't want to appear too hopeful, in case she didn't win. But her heart beat wildly against her ribcage, betraying her plan. She was bubbling over with hope, just by knowing she'd made a positive impression on someone highly influential that day. Despite her inner voice of self-loathing – reminding her she shouldn't ever think she'd be more than a mere farm girl, she pushed it aside, desiring to believe the impossible – her dreams becoming a reality.

## Chapter Eight

Tilly suppressed the urge to hoop and holler when Starla Hennessee recited her name as the first place winner. Afterward, Mrs. Jacobs had taken her to dine at a fancy steakhouse to celebrate. Tilly gingerly held the edges of the check between her right thumb and left index finger. It'd been made out to her from the art foundation. Starla's eloquent handwriting was scrawled across the paper; Tilly thought her own name hadn't appeared so intricate before.

"Tilly-Ann, I cannot tell you how proud I am of you," Rosalie remarked, patting her knee gently.

Tilly gazed up at the doctor's wife. They were still a 30 minute drive from home. After winning the cash prize, she felt her confidence soaring. She glided her tongue across her lower lip, attempting to build her resolve. What she was about to ask would take courage.

"Mrs. Jacob's, I appreciate you investing your time in me.

I would've never received an opportunity like this if it weren't for you. Having this chance made me realize how much I'd like to go back to school and work towards my high school diploma. Pa claims he needs my help on the farm, but Nadine will be starting school in the fall. I'd just need a backup plan for Theresa..." She trailed off, realizing without a place for Theresa to go, she'd have no choice but to stay home.

As the car stopped at a railroad crossing, Rosalie opted to speak. "I'm proud of you for having the courage to tell me that. You're too bright of a girl to be stuck at home tending to your family's farm all day. Don't worry, I'll watch Theresa. You and Nadine can ride the bus to our house to complete your homework, in the afternoon. It'll be swell to have some young people in our home after all these years. I know Alexander won't mind."

Tilly's eyes transformed into two twin saucers. Flabbergasted, she replied, "are you serious!?"

"As a heart attack, and don't you worry about your father. Let me reason with him," she instructed.

Tilly nodded amicably, relieved she wouldn't be the one to face off with her father. His anger could flare up instantaneously, and she wasn't sure if her request to finish school would bode well for her. Her daddy had quit school in the third grade, to work the fields, and he saw no need for a formal education. However, the farm life was all he'd ever known, so she couldn't expect him to understand. She silently sent up a prayer to God, asking him to soften her father's heart concerning the matter.

The moment she'd arrived home, Mrs. Jacobs collected her check. As much as she'd relish bragging to her father about her accomplishments, they'd decided it would be best to keep him out of the loop. The first thing he'd wish to do was take the check and invest it in the farm. Rosalie's idea was to set the money aside for Tilly's college fund. Rosalie had promised they'd head to the bank on Monday and open her a savings account.

When they'd entered the house, she was greeted by two rambunctious girls, which smothered her with kisses. Bart Matthews had entered the kitchen next, pulling her into a tight hug. "You sure look pretty. Mrs. Jacobs buy you some new clothes?" he asked.

"Just a couple of dresses," she replied modestly. Her father didn't take pride in asking others for help, so there was no way she was about to enlighten him about the expensive steak dinner Rosalie had treated her to.

"Well, you look fine in 'em, Pumpkin." He smiled gently, kissing her forehead affectionately. Rosalie nodded in her direction – their signal for her to head upstairs.

Tilly grabbed her suitcase, smiling brilliantly at her Father. "Thanks, Daddy, I believe I'm going to take my stuff upstairs. I've got a couple of souvenirs for the girls." She winked at her sisters, their faces lighting up like Christmas lights. She hugged Rosalie quickly, thanking her for her a wonderful time before bounding up the stairs – little feet pattering behind her.

The warm atmosphere within the room grew icy. Bart sauntered to the fridge, grabbing himself a pitcher of water. "Would you like some, Mrs. Jacobs? Finest tap water in the county," he taunted, pouring himself a glass and taking a sip.

"No, thank you," she politely declined. "But I do have a request to make of you."

"And what would that be?" Water dribbled down his beard as he granted her his undivided attention.

"Tilly confided in me during our trip, and told me she'd like to return to school. I told her she and Nadine can get off the bus at our house. I'll help them with their homework and keep Theresa during the day while they're both in school," she supplied.

Bart clacked his glass onto the counter with an angry thud. “No, I need Tilly here on the farm!” he snapped, waggling his index finger at the front door.

Rosalie placed a hand on her elegant hip. “So, you're going to subject her to a life filled with no opportunities, suppress her dreams and ambitions until there's nothing left!? We live in different times now, Bart. The world is expanding, and Tilly has more opportunities, now, than we ever did back then. Your daughter is bright, and she wants an education. Don't snuff out the little hope which remains in her heart. She became a mother to her sisters, but they're growing up. There's no reason for her to remain on this farm forever if she doesn't wish it!" she asserted.

Bart hung his head guiltily. Tilly had always done whatever he'd asked of her without putting up a fight. He knew he was being ridiculous. He knew he and the boys could manage without her; he supposed relinquishing his control would be best. Deep down he was afraid of losing her, just as he had her mother. It was so hard for him to let go, though he knew it was time.

Bart sighed, scratching his beard. “Fine, but you're in

charge of her.  If she gets in any trouble, it's on you," he relented, though they both knew she wouldn't.

Tilly had secretly been listening to their exchange from the stairwell.  Her heart skipped a beat in anticipation.  As small as it would seem to others, it was a gigantic leap for her.  Her life was finally headed in the right direction, and the world was at her fingertips.  She knew God had faithfully answered her prayer, and with him by her side, she knew there wasn't anything she couldn't accomplish.

## Chapter Nine

The Sunday before school started, Tilly had gone to visit Trina. They'd prepared a picnic lunch and lay sprawled out in front of the duck pond. Sammi, Trina's orange tabby, lazed on the blanket with them. She purred contentedly as Trina scratched behind her ears. "I'm really glad you're coming back to school with us, Tilly-Ann."

Tilly faced her friend on the blanket, smiling serenely. "Me too, Trina. I just hope I'm able to catch up. I haven't attended school since the seventh grade, and the school board decided to place me in the grade appropriate for my age. They gave me a grade level entry exam, and I miraculously aced it. Eleventh grade sounds rigorous, though," Tilly groaned, grabbing a nearby dandelion and blowing away the remaining seeds. A few bits of white fluff got caught in Sammi's whiskers, and she sneezed.

Trina sat up, shaking her head – her red braid swishing

back and forth. “You'll excel at whatever you do. If Red Langston can skip through each grade then you should have no problem.”

Tilly chuckled as the image of the brutish, sandy-blond haired boy emerged in her mind. He missed school all of the time, but he kept growing so tall that the teachers kept passing him. He'd often picked fights in the schoolyard with the other kids, making him a liability. Easing him into graduation was the only way to ensure the other students' safety.

“Except I'm not brawny or tall,” Tilly deadpanned.

Trina shrugged. “Nah, you're as delicate as a daisy, but you do have brains, and brains will get you further than brawn.”

“Unless you're Red Langston!” They remarked simultaneously. “Jinx!” They waggled a finger in each others' faces before exploding into a fit of giggles. Tilly laughed until her sides ached. When they managed to compose themselves, Trina grabbed Tilly's hand, interlacing their fingers as they'd often done when they were younger. They watched as a gentle breeze rippled the duck pond – the sun beginning to set behind the mountains. Oranges, reds, pinks, purples, and golds dotted the sky, rendering Tilly breathless as she reminisced about the day she'd painted her first sunset. Life had changed so much for her since then, and she exuberantly anticipated the next step, God had planned for her. There remained two years left of high school, but then what? Would she pursue a college degree or continue to look after the farm? The possibilities were endless, but she decided taking life one day at a time was the best approach. Each day must be lived to its fullest and each presented opportunities which would never arise again. She would capture each breath with purpose and live with expectancy, that whatever God had planned for her would far exceed her own dreams.

## Chapter Ten

Tilly chewed on her lower lip in anticipation, as she held Nadine's dainty hand, awaiting the school bus to arrive. They'd already dropped Theresa off with the Jacobs. She'd cried the entire way there, clinging to Tilly like a second skin, begging to go to school with them. She was exceptionally bright for her age and would join her and her sister the following year. Hopefully, she wouldn't give the middle-aged couple too much trouble.

As the bus pulled up, dust swirling behind its tires, Tilly wiped a bead of sweat from her brow. She held Nadine's hand as they ascended the steps; Tilly scanned the other seats as the doors creak shut behind them. A sea of unfamiliar faces greeted her. Most of the children riding her bus appeared to be in grammar school. She escorted Nadine to a seat closer to the front, allowing her to sit beside the window. Her sweet sister chatted animatedly as they wove around country roads. Nadine was thrilled about her first day of school, and Tilly prayed she made lots of friends and adored her new teacher. The bus halted in front of a building with chipped paint and leaking roofs. The school was nearly rundown, but the county couldn't afford to build another one. All twelve grades were contained in one building. The town's population was small, which meant one teacher taught each grade. The kids you began first grade with would be who you were stuck with until high school graduation. Tilly had walked Nadine to her first grade class. She'd kissed her older sister's cheek before hurriedly skipping away to meet her classmates. Mrs. Hodges was her teacher – a plump woman with salt and pepper hair. She exuded great belly-laughs and warm hugs. All children typically adored her, and she would forever remain one of Tilly's favorite teachers. She smiled and waved at her former teacher before sauntering down the hall to find her own class. She swallowed hard as she entered the classroom. Thirteen desks were already occupied when she took one next to Trina. She mouthed a 'thank you' to her friend for graciously saving her a seat. She could feel her former classmates' eyes on her, staring a hole through the back of her head. It was as if she were an apparition, but she couldn't blame them. She was scarcely around any of the townsfolk, besides her family, the Jacobs, and Trina. Her father had practically kept her isolated from the world since her mother's passing, and she did her best not to resent him for it. She'd missed out on dozens of socials and hadn't even went out on her first date, thanks to his overprotective nature.

In her mind, she determined to change all of that, as Mr. Jones – a balding man around sixty – stalked into the room. She pulled her black and white composition book from her backpack, scribbling down notes from his first lecture. He'd quickly introduced himself before jumping into their first lesson. Thankfully she'd had no trouble keeping up, and by lunch time she felt confident with the beginning material.

She and Trina had sat beneath a shady oak behind the school during lunch. Trina picked off pieces of her peanut butter sandwich, tossing a piece of it to a nearby robin.

"I wish summer break wasn't over, it went by too fast," Trina huffed, biting into her apple. She licked the juice from her upper lip, complaining about Mr. Jones monotone and him already assigning homework on the first day.

"I'm just thankful to be back in school, having conversations with people my own age. Caleb is about as intelligent as a mule's behind and the girls still care too much about their dollies for my own good," Tilly returned, sipping from her milk carton.

Trina snorted in amusement. "It's funny how we have two different perceptions about these matters."

Tilly noted how her cheeks flushed with color as she gazed intently at the robin, as if her words held a double meaning. "I have an inkling this has more to do than with us starting back to school," she remarked skeptically.

"I'm not sure I know what you're talking about," Trina mumbled, feigning ignorance.

Tilly furrowed a delicate brow. "I poked fun at Caleb's lack of intellect and commented on how glad I was to be back within our social circle. You said it was funny how we hold two different perceptions, and I have a feeling by the blush discoloring your cheeks, you didn't mean the latter."

Trina squirmed at her accusation, clenching a handful of her floral dress within her hands and wringing it together uncomfortably. "I have no idea what you're inferring, Tilly-Ann, but you're wrong." She diverted her gaze towards the bouncing robin, opting to ignore her friend's clever accusation.

Tilly's eyes widened with realization. She gasped, jumping to her feet. "You like Caleb!?"

Trina whipped her head around, her eyes filled with panic. "Pipe down, Tilly, don't announce it to the entire student body!" she hissed in displeasure.

Tilly held her hands up in response. "Okay, I'm sorry, but how long has this been going on!? And why am I just finding out, now!?" she demanded.

Trina sighed exasperatedly, closing the distance between them. She placed her hands on Tilly's shoulders, gazing deeply into her eyes. "Just since the beginning of this summer. I wanted to tell you, but I was afraid you might be upset. He's your brother and all, and I didn't want to cross into any forbidden territory."

Tilly's lips twitched into a Cheshire grin as she hugged Trina tightly, giggling girlishly. "Why would you think I'd be upset!? I'm happy for you, though I'll never understand the appeal you see in courting my brother." She made fake gagging noises, eliciting a playful smack on the head from Trina.

"You better not tell a soul, Tilly-Ann," Trina forewarned.

"I won't, cross my heart," Tilly vowed, making a finger cross symbol in front of her chest.

"Thank you," Trina beamed, relief flooding her features.

The conversation halted as the bell rang, signaling it was

time for everyone to return to their classes. The high school kids meandered inside, stopping in the hallways to chat minutes before the next bell. Tilly settled back into her seat alongside Trina. The rest of the day sped by in a blur, and when the final bell rang, she dropped by Nadine's classroom to retrieve her. The first grader chatted non-stop about her exciting first day and how she couldn't wait to go back tomorrow.

When they'd arrived at the Jacobs' residence, Rosalie had supper prepared for them. They ate a hearty meal before beginning their homework. Theresa demanded to know every miniscule detail about Nadine's day. Tilly attempted to focus on an algebra problem, glancing over the notes Mr. Jones had written on the board for them to copy. It had taken her several hours to complete her homework because her academic skills needed brushing up. She knew she was rusty, yet she persevered through it. It was half-past seven when they arrived home. The girls were ready to pass out, so Tilly tucked them in. The sink was filled with dirty dishes, and the table was covered in scraps of food.

“Darn it,” Tilly groaned, suddenly feeling lethargic as she eyed the mountain of dishware and cutlery her father and brothers had left her to tidy up.

She rolled up her sleeves, ready to begin the cumbersome chore when she felt someone gently touch her shoulder. She stiffened, turning to meet her father's gaze. “I'm sorry we're late, but I had a lot of homework, and I promise to clean this up before I go to bed,” she stammered.

Bart shook his head, gently shoving her aside. “Nah, you go and relax, Pumpkin. I'll do the dishes. I know you've worked hard today.”

Tilly was startled by his unusual, generous offer but wasn't about to deter him. Instead, she kissed his scruffy cheek. “Thanks, Pa,” she remarked before bounding up the stairs. Tilly crept quietly into her bedroom, bypassing her snoozing sisters. She grabbed a blank canvas and her paint set. It was nearing dusk, and the sky was splattered in an infinite palette of indescribable, brilliant hues. Tilly settled down on the front steps and began to paint her second sunset. Once she'd finished it, her fingers pleasantly ached and her paints splattered the stoop. She marveled at her finished piece, beaming from ear to ear. Compared to her last one, she'd definitely honed in on her skills. This one wouldn't hang in the kitchen beside her first one. Despite her improvement, she didn't cherish it as she did the sunset with smudged colors her baby sister had fawned over. This one was better, but the one in her kitchen was her – raw and imperfect, embodied with magnificent color. She would gift this one to Mr. and Mrs. Jacobs – allow other people to derive joy from her unforeseen talent. Tilly Matthews would paint many sunsets during her lifetime – each one better than the last. However, only one would be truly significant to her – the one God inspired her to paint and show her how priceless and beautiful she was to him.

## Chapter Eleven

Since her mother's death, Tilly's relationship with God had been hot and cold. The trauma she'd suffered from losing her mother at a young age made her resent her Creator most of the time. However, here of late, she found herself yearning to know more about the God her mother had spent hours praying to and abundantly adored. It all began one, crisp autumn morning. It was Sunday, and Tilly was scurrying about the farm, attempting to finish her chores before breakfast. Her father allowed her to be lax during the week because he knew she had school work to complete, but during the weekend she was required to pull her weight around the farm. They were dreadfully busy, especially with the fall harvest swiftly approaching. She hauled a bucket filled with fresh water from the well towards the pig stall. As she poured the bucket's contents into the watering trough, she felt two small arms wrap around her. Tilly spun around, blinking owlishly when she saw

Nadine and Theresa dressed in their Sunday best.

“Why are you all dressed up for, girls?” Tilly inquired, perching a hand on her petite hip.

“We wanna go to church,” Theresa piped up, rocking back and forth on her heels.

“Yeah, Marcus, from my class told me they're having a potluck after church, and he said they'll be all kinds of delicious goodies,” Nadine chimed in.

Tilly felt a pang of guilt seize her chest from Nadine's admission. She'd never truly took her sisters to church regularly since their mother's passing. She didn't read the Bible to them as their Mother had done for her. Tilly's mind flashed back to the final day she'd spent with her mother, praying in her bedroom. Mother's alabaster box had sat on the bed, filled with hundreds of her prayer requests. She'd prayed that day for Tilly to grow into a God-fearing woman. Conviction washed over her; she knew she wasn't being the example her sisters needed nor living the life her Mother desired her to. There was no use in putting it off any longer. Today was as good as any to turn over a new leaf.

Tilly placed the bucket on the ground, dusting her hands on her apron as two pairs of eyes peered hopefully at her. “Let me go in and change real quick, and we'll head to church."

Collective cheers erupted inside the barn as Tilly raced towards the house. She sprinted up the stairs to her bedroom and quickly changed into a pale blue cotton dress. She combed her hair and tied back her waterfall curls in a neat ribbon. Toeing into her black polished shoes, she raced out the door where the pair of sisters waited on the porch.

"You look pretty, Sissy!" Theresa beamed, blowing her a kiss.

Tilly grinned, pretending to catch it. "Let's hurry or we'll be late!"

She looped her arms through theirs, and they began the mile trek to the chapel. Tilly hadn't bothered telling her father where they were headed. He and her brothers were deep in the fields, and she hadn't had time to signal them. Hopefully the service would be short, and they would be back home before any of the others noticed their absence. When they arrived, church had already started. They slipped into a back pew, unnoticed. Reverend Vann stood at the podium with his Bible open, reading from Matthew about Jesus' account in Gethsemane. The reverend poured out his heart with each spoken word, speaking about how Jesus prayed so fervently that his sweat became great drops of blood. He told how Jesus faced deep anguish within his own soul as he made the decision to go to Calvary and die on a cross for all of humanity's sins. One of his beloved disciples betrayed him, and the rest deserted him. He was mocked and spat upon by the religious teachers of the law and those who'd reverenced him mere days before. He was tortured, beaten, and bruised for our transgressions, the minister had said. Tilly's mind filled with vivid images of each account the reverend spoke of. Her heart was heavy and tears spilled over her lashes when he gave the altar call, asking if anyone wished to be saved and accept Jesus as their personal Savior. Tilly's feet felt like lead as she trudged down the aisle – the weight of her guilt and sin heavy on her heart.

As she collapsed in front of the altar, her body trembling as she sobbed, Tilly never realized she needed saving more than in that moment. She poured her heart out to God, her lips quivering as she repented of every sin which came to mind. She vowed to live her life fully for him from that day forward, no matter what the cost. Small hands touched her backside as she prayed, mumbling comforting words she couldn't quite decipher. She realized her sisters had followed her to the altar, concerned when she'd left them behind, but this only prompted her to pray harder.

That Sunday morning, Tilly-Ann Matthews became a citizen of the Kingdom of Heaven. Reverend Vann grinned from ear to ear as he recounted the prayer he'd prayed over the distraught girl he'd met in the cemetery all those years ago. This time, he prayed another, he prayed a fiery passion for serving Christ would consume her soul, and she would blaze a trail for others to follow towards her beloved Savior. God heard the reverend's prayers once again as a teary-eyed young woman gave her heart to him.

He would mold her heart into a heart like his, including gathering up the bitter ashes of her broken past – transforming them into something far more beautiful than she would ever be able to comprehend. He would use all the pain and heartache she'd endured for his glory; he would renew her strength, and she would walk boldly with him for the rest of her days.

## Chapter Twelve

Since that Sunday morning, Tilly's life hadn't been the same. Her heart felt lighter, and she was overwhelmed with such inconceivable joy. She hadn't told her father, but he hadn't even noticed they were missing the day they'd decided to go to church. They'd stayed for the potluck and had their bellies filled, but Tilly noted how full her soul felt as well. She had sneaked into her parents' bedroom when her father was scarce and located her mother's Bible. She'd began to study it whenever she had the time, poring over it during the late hours of the night by candlelight as her sisters slept. Her hunger to know more couldn't be sated. Once, she'd discreetly attempted to read it during one of Mr. Jones lectures. Unfortunately, he'd caught her and confiscated her precious text until the end of the day. She'd been grateful once he'd returned it, gently reprimanding her for reading during class. He'd told her to keep it at home where it belonged; reminding her God wanted her to be successful in all her endeavors, which meant she had to stay focused on her studies if she wished to graduate. Tilly knew he was right, so she began to study harder than ever before. Near the end of her junior year, Mr. Jones had coerced her to meet with him a few minutes during lunch break. He'd sat behind his desk, hands poised on a stack of graded papers in front of him.

"You wished to speak with me, Mr. Jones?" Tilly stood in front of his desk, shifting from one foot to the other, nervously.

"Yes, Ms. Matthews, you've portrayed exceptional progress since jumping back into school, and I believe you have the ability to do more than procure your high school diploma. I believe you have the potential for college, and I think you should apply for an academic scholarship," he said.

"Me!? College? I have the farm and -"

Mr. Jones held up his hand to silence her. "It's just something to think about, Ms. Matthews. There's no need in getting all in a frenzy. Contemplate it a few days, and if you're interested, I can help you with the application process."

Mr. Jones smiled encouragingly, and Tilly's shoulders relaxed. "Thank you, Mr. Jones," she simply stated, leaving him to have lunch with Trina.

Tilly had never imagined college as a possibility for

herself. Mrs. Jacobs had stowed away her prize money in an account nearly a year ago.

The nearest university was over and hour away from home. It was far, considering she didn't own a car, meaning she couldn't commute or come home on the weekends. She was certain Mrs. Jacobs wouldn't mind retrieving her for the holidays, but those matters were trivial compared to what she would be leaving behind – two small girls who counted on her for everything. She sensed her academic dreams wilt as she thought of their cherub faces. If Mother was still around, perhaps she could have gone to college, but it wouldn't be happening now, not ever.

Tilly had politely declined Mr. Jones offer but continued to strive to do her best in school. She was proud of her hard work. and when she received her final report card before school ended for the summer, she was pleasantly surprised to see she'd made the honor roll.

When she'd showed her report card to Mrs. Jacobs, she'd insisted they celebrate. She and her husband had taken Tilly to a popular eatery in a bigger town and had purchased her some new Sunday attire – including new shoes. It hadn't been the only surprise awaiting her that evening. Starla Hennessee – the art critic from the gallery showing the prior year had written her a personal letter, requesting she arrange a showcase of her best pieces for that year's event.

"What should I choose from!?" Tilly had asked Mrs. Jacobs, giddily.

"You should choose the pieces closest to your heart, not your most immaculate, but the ones you painted during the times you needed to release a rush of emotions," Mrs. Jacobs had told her.

Tilly's mind buzzed with anticipation as she mulled over which paintings would be appropriate for the gallery show. She didn't want to choose mediocre art; she knew Starla would be less than impressed if she did, and probably regret requesting she arrange a showcase. The first painting which emerged within her mind to enter made her shake her head at the notion. The sunset, with its smudged spectrum of colors demanded to be on display. It held a lot of sentimental value to her, but she couldn't say others would see past its imperfections. Despite her hesitation, she decided to follow Mrs. Jacobs advice and submit it, regardless of what others thought. Her paintings told a story, and it was high time people heard it. Perhaps her art would compel others to share their stories, and help those trudging through their own pain to heal. What she couldn't find the words to say, echoed loudly with each stroke of her brush. People connected deeply with emotions and feelings, and Tilly prayed they would be enraptured by her art, so they might have the opportunity to speak with her and be made whole as she had.

## Chapter Thirteen

One summer evening, after her chores were complete, Tilly sat on the front steps, drinking a glass of cool, tart lemonade. She swiped tendrils of sweat soaked curls from her eyes. Suddenly, Caleb plopped down beside her, snatching the glass from her hands and draining its contents.

"Hey!" Tilly growled, shoving him.

He grinned mischievously, jabbing her hard in the ribs. "That's no way to greet your favorite brother, now is it?"

"You're definitely not my favorite brother and never will be," she clarified, snatching the empty glass from his hands and placing it behind her.

Caleb shrugged. "Ah, well, buttering you up isn't why I'm here any how," he added, removing his straw hat and scrubbing his hand through his unruly blond curls.

"Then why are you here?" Tilly furrowed a brow, analyzing him closely, musing over why he was wasting her time.

Caleb's shoulders sagged and his baby blues seemed troubled. "Trina said she doesn't want us to go steady if I'm not willing to be a follower of Christ. She wants me to go to church with her and become a man of God. You know I've been turned off by religion since Ma died..." he trailed off, averting his gaze towards the horizon.

Tilly was stunned by his revelation. He'd come to her for advice – a matter which dealt with her best friend. She closed her eyes, silently praying for God to give her the words her brother needed to hear.

"I resented God for a long time after losing, Ma, but it's like he kept relentlessly pursuing my heart. He didn't stop until I fully surrendered. I guess you know I've been sneaking the girls to church on Sundays," she admitted sheepishly.

Caleb leveled her with a hard glance. "Yeah, all of us know, but Pa drinks like a fish, and he doesn't notice much. The boys and I have been picking up his slack," he remarked, his voice laced with agitation.

"I'm sorry I hadn't noticed. Going to school and taking care of our sisters has become my first priority," she admitted, feeling a wave of guilt consume her for being unobservant of their father's deteriorating condition.

Caleb plucked a milkweed from his shirt pocket, sticking it between his chapped lips. "You ain't got nothin' to be sorry for. I don't ever say it, but I'm real proud of you for holding things together these last few years. Without you, this family would've already fallen apart." He patted her back twice before standing, his declaration shaking her to the core. Caleb Matthews – her brother which had relentlessly teased her their entire lives - had just paid her one of the highest compliments she'd ever received.

"Thanks, Caleb," she remarked, stifling back tears which threatened to fall.

"You're welcome, Sis," he smiled wryly, tossing the milkweed aside. He stood, brushing the dirt off his jeans. "Reckon I'll give this church thing a try Sunday."

"I hope you will." Tilly smiled proudly as she watched him straighten his hat. He stood, ruffling her curls affectionately before taking his leave. That Sunday, Caleb came as promised, and he continued to be at each service until he was making the most significant commitment he would ever make – accepting Jesus as his personal savior.

Brother and Sister decided to be baptized together that

summer – down at the local creek. Cold water dripped from their clothes as their souls became white as freshly fallen snow.

"So, I guess this what Mama was talking about all along," he commented later that afternoon, after their bellies had been filled, and the lightning bugs dotted the fields.

"What?" Tilly inquired, meeting his gaze.

"My soul feels sanctified; it feels whole, like I found my missing piece or something," he added, leaning against the door frame.

"You've made a change, and you're feeling it on the inside. Jesus has came in and cleaned up all that grime and rot festering on the inside of you," she replied.

"If I'd only known how refreshing this felt, I would've made the change a lot sooner," he said, bowing his head regretfully.

Tilly clasped her older brother's shoulder reassuringly. "You've made the change and that's what counts. We'll see her again one day, you know. I bet she's up there grinning ear to ear, proud of the both of us."

Caleb shot her a meek smile. "Yeah, you know, I'm real sorry for how I've treated you these last few years. I should have helped you out more with the girls, but I didn't."

"The monumental thing about Jesus forgiving me is that I

now have the ability to truly forgive you, Caleb. And I do, I truly do," she said, leaning upwards to press a kiss against the stubble along his jaw. He wrapped his arm around her shoulders, holding her close. "Let's allow this to be a new beginning for the both of us."

"Amen," Tilly remarked, observing the glittering stars which had began to flicker above them – in awe of her Savior and his overwhelming majesty.

## Chapter Fourteen

When the day of Tilly's gallery showcase arrived, she found herself feeling frazzled and unprepared. Were her pieces show worthy? Should she have picked artwork which was more impressionable? She'd handpicked eight paintings, with Mrs. Jacobs and Trina's help – of course. Two of them were landscapes, which depicted scenery behind her childhood home. One was a portrait of Nadine and Theresa eating homemade ice cream. The fourth was Trina, holding her orange tabby-cat Sammi, beside the duck pond. A painting of the country church she'd grown up in, surrounded by wildflowers during the heart of spring took the fifth spot. Six and seven were far more personal to Tilly, as they were of her mother. One portrayed her sitting in her favorite rocking chair, her Holy Bible open – nestled in her lap. The other was of her kneeling at her bedside, hands folded in prayer – the alabaster box resting in front of her. Mrs Jacobs had prodded her about the significance of the box, but Tilly had only mentioned it was a prop she felt like adding. No one knew about the box, tucked away safely in the confines of her mother's closet. That box meant everything to her, it was a secret Mother had shared with her on her final day of life. The final piece she'd chosen was her beloved sunset – imperfect but her most cherished painting.

Tilly had been granted her own personal space to display her paintings. She'd grouped them together in a tidy row. Starla Hennessee had stopped by before the judging began. Starla's silver hair was pulled back in a neat bun and her age lines crinkled when she smiled, as she admired each of Tilly's paintings.

"My word! I cannot believe how much you've improved since last summer! Such a God-given talent you've been bestowed with, indeed!" she fawned over them, until she reached the last painting.

"I believe it was a grand idea to choose a novice painting to add to your gallery. It clearly shows how much you've advanced in your skills. I'm certain the other art critics will simply adore what you have decided to share with us!" Starla beamed proudly, her clipboard clasped at her waist.

"Thank you, Mrs. Hennessee," Tilly remarked humbly, her

cheeks blooming with heat from all of the flattery.

Trina and Caleb had accompanied her to the gallery this year, while Mrs. Jacobs babysat the girls. The event would last most of the day, meaning they would have tired out quickly. They'd sent her off with multiple kisses for good luck.

Caleb had worn his Sunday best; Trina remained close to his side, adorned in her modest, periwinkle ankle-length dress. She'd never witnessed her brother look at anyone the way he had Trina. It made her own heart ache with something deeply unfamiliar. One year left of school meant they would probably marry soon. Caleb had hinted about proposing on multiple occasions, lately. Boys her age barely gave Tilly a second glance. She'd deemed herself as plain and invisible, but it mattered little. After graduation she'd be expected to resume her duties on the farm and keep watching after the girls. The weight of her responsibilities settled on her chest like an anvil.

"Tilly, are you alright? You're frowning," Trina observed, her face becoming overcast with concern.

"No! I'm fine! Just nervous," Tilly downplayed, plastering on her most genuine smile.

Trina's expression relaxed. "Good, but you shouldn't be. You're talented, and your artwork speaks for itself."

Trina's reassurance soothed her frayed emotions. She opted to concentrate on her blessings instead of what she was lacking. Caleb shot her a knowing look. He knew she was troubled and putting up a front, but she was grateful he hadn't patronized her about it.

The time passed by swiftly, and Tilly managed to sell three of her paintings before the end of the day. The churchyard filled with wildflowers, her sister's ice cream portrait, and the one of her mother reading her Bible had all sold. Starla had stopped back by at the end of the show to congratulate her on her successes. Selling three paintings at your first gallery showcase was apparently an unprecedented feat. She'd carried the others back home, stowed them away safely, and counted her earnings. One hundred and fifty dollars was a decent profit for a novice artist.

Tilly had handed her earnings off to Mrs. Jacobs for safe keeping. She was stunned when she received a letter from Starla Hennessee three short weeks later, inviting to her a private luncheon for all of the artists which had been at the showcase. She'd also requested Tilly bring the painting of Mother praying at her bedside because she desired to purchase it for herself.

Overwhelmed by God's goodness to her on this ordinary day made her raise her hands in worship to the One who had granted her all of these wonderful gifts. Life was grand, and she was grateful to be alive.

## Chapter Fifteen

Tilly's suspicions had been correct. Caleb proposed to Trina three days before their senior year began. Trina's parents approved of the match, but her daddy said she would have to wait until graduation before they tied the knot. Tilly was elated for the pair, and having her childhood best friend as her new sister-in-law was merely an added bonus. Despite their celebration, Tilly felt a tinge of bitterness begin to spurn within her. It coiled around her heart like a serpent, squeezing the life out of her whenever she imagined herself growing into an old spinster. She began to paint more, poring over her studies endlessly, hoping it would fill the gaping hole within her heart. If anything, busying herself only numbed it. For the first time in her eighteen years, she desired a husband. She didn't want to spend the remainder of her life tied to this farm. No, she yearned for her own life and family. She began to pray earnestly for God to fulfill her request, however he remained silent to her pleas it seemed.

She'd shared the matter with, Mrs. Jacobs, over tea one afternoon. The auburn haired woman smiled fondly at her, patting her hand from across the table. “It's perfectly normal for a young lady to desire those things, Tilly-Ann, but you shouldn't put those longings before God. He deserves your heart more than anyone and can love you more deeply than any mortal man ever will. No, you need to lay your desire of marriage on the altar and tell God that even if he doesn't see fit to send you a husband, you'll still serve him with all of your heart. I know it's a scary thought to your young mind, but you aren't an old maid. If God truly has someone for you, then he'll bring you both together in his timing,” Mrs. Jacobs had responded.

Despite her misgivings, Tilly knew Mrs. Jacobs was right. God knew what was best for her, including if she needed a mate. She'd prayed and asked God to give her the desires of his heart, and if he had someone for her, to make it plain as day.

Tilly would often gaze at her local prospects. Their town was small, and most of the boys in her senior class were too immature for her tastes. She'd given up on any of them possibly being the one.

She'd attended Starla's luncheon in the fall, presenting her with the painting of her mother praying as she'd requested. The event was held at her own private estates. Starla had provided her with a bus ticket, so she could attend the gathering. Near the end of the meal, Starla had requested Tilly join her in her office. The room was filled with dozens of pieces, painted by artists all across the globe. Starla sat behind a mahogany desk, her hands folded neatly in front of her.

"You should sit, Tilly," Starla insisted, gesticulating to the leather back chair.

"Yes, Mam," Tilly obliged, deciding to take the chair to the left of her.

Starla smiled kindly at the young woman, her eyes sparkling with mirth. "How did you find the luncheon?"

"It was excellent, Mam," Tilly stammered, "I greatly appreciate you inviting me."

Starla's grin widened. "Oh! I can't hold it in any longer, Tilly! I didn't invite you here just to enjoy some fancy cuisine. The reason you're in my office is because I cherish you so much. Your exuberance and raw talent remind me of myself when I was younger. I've been retired from the art world for many years, but I'd like to contribute to your future, Tilly. I see great potential in you, which is why I'd like to become your patron!"

Tilly's heart slammed into her ribcage as she attempted to absorb the other woman's words. "My patron? What does that entail!?"

"It means I'll be funding your education for art school. You can live here with me in my manor and attend school at the local university, nearby. After you graduate, you can expect your art career to soar," Starla explained, moving her hands upwards – her eyes alight with enthusiasm.

Tilly's heart beat with anticipation for a fleeting moment. Starla had just presented her with the opportunity of a lifetime, but she felt it slip through her grasp in wisps of smoke. There were so many reasons why she couldn't accept her offer. Two cherub faces surfaced within her mind – faces she cared deeply for – her baby sisters. Tilly's countenance immediately fell. Starla frowned.

"I'm not liking the despondency permeating your features, Darling. Why the long face?" Starla inquired gently.

Tilly locked gazes with the artist, tears threatening to fall. "Your offer is a dream come true, and I can't thank you enough, but when Mother passed away, I became the woman of the house, and I have two little girls which depend upon me greatly."

Starla stood and rounded her desk. She held her arms open to the young woman, and Tilly found herself craving comfort she barely received. She embraced the highborn, art critic, allowing herself to be consoled. For a moment, she allowed herself to imagine they were Mother's arms holding her, reminding her that everything would turn out okay.

Starla released her from her grasp, placing her pointer finger under Tilly's chin and tilting her face upwards. "You don't have to say yes to my offer today, but I don't want you to disregard it either. In a few years, your sisters will be old enough to fend for themselves. When you feel that day has arrived, you give me a call, or write to me, and I'll send you another bus ticket. You'll come and stay with me and live under my patronage."

Tilly nodded amicably. "I will, I promise. You have my word."

Starla hugged the young woman again, kissing her brow lightly. "Take care of yourself, Darling, and stay in touch."

"I will," Tilly vowed before making her departure.

During the bus ride home, Tilly meditated on Romans 8:28, which stated," God works for the good of those who love him, who have been called according to his purpose." Tilly knew she'd been called according to his purpose, even if she wasn't exactly certain what it entailed.

## Chapter Sixteen

A smattering of cumulus clouds dotted a crisp, blue sky. It was mid-October, and autumn leaves blanketed the countryside in an array of colors. Tilly adored fall. It was her favorite season, and she supposed it was because it was Mother's, too. Bart Matthews had planted several rows of pumpkins to take to the Farmer's Market.

Tilly was nonplussed to spy a tall, lanky gentleman placing several pumpkins into a wheelbarrow when she arrived home from school that evening. He wore a straw hat, but Tilly could see dark curls peeking from beneath it. She attempted to place him, but she came to the realization she'd never seen him before.

She padded into the house, the screen door swinging behind her as she entered the kitchen. Caleb stood by the sink, washing his hands.

"Who's that fellow outside in the pumpkin patch?" Tilly inquired, laying her school satchel on the table.

Caleb dried his hands on a dishtowel, meeting her gaze. "He's Reverend Vann's nephew, he arrived in town a few days ago. He was walking down the road and saw we had pumpkins. He stopped by and asked if he could pick a few for the church's upcoming harvest festival. He was rolling a cart, so I guess he was looking for some. We chatted a bit; apparently he's moved in with the reverend. He's going to be assisting him from now on, said his health has been declining for awhile. He doesn't have any children or close kin, so Tobias moved here to keep an eye on him," Caleb illuminated.

"Tobias?" Tilly blinked owlishly.

Caleb shoved his hands in his pockets. "Yeah, he introduced himself as Tobias Gable."

Tilly mused over his name for a moment – Tobias Gable. It was no secret the reverend's health had been waning for the last several months. Sometimes he was too ill to deliver his weekly sermon. Hopefully his nephew would see to it that he took his medication properly and took better care of himself.

She startled when she heard a knock at the front door. "Care to get that?" Caleb asked, stirring a pitcher of sweet tea he'd just made.

Tilly nodded, sprinting to the door. She wrenched it open to find a man with soulful sable eyes staring back at her. Raven curls peeped beneath his straw hat, and he gazed at her a moment, both spellbound.

Tilly managed to find her voice. “You must be Tobias.”

A smile crinkled at the edges of his mouth as he reached out his hand for a shake. Tilly reluctantly took it, feeling her heart flutter madly in her chest as his calloused digits grazed her fingertips. “You'd be correct, Miss -”

“ - Matilda Matthews, I mean, Tilly. Mostly everyone around here calls me Tilly, though,” she stammered, heat blooming to her cheeks as she intently studied his handsome face. Ruddy cheeks, an aquiline nose, twin blue eyes she could easily become enraptured in.

Tobias grinned at her introduction. “It's a pleasure to meet you, Matilda Matthews.” Tilly noted his thick southern drawl – alluring and as smooth as butter.

After releasing her hand, Tobias reached into his overall's pocket, handing her a wad of crumpled bills. “I hope this will be enough to cover the pumpkins.”

Tilly shook her head, pushing the money back into his

hand. “No, my brother said you were gathering them for the harvest festival for church. Consider it a donation.”

“You really should take the money; I was raised on a farm myself, and I know how much hard work it takes to grow anything,” he insisted.

Tilly wavered – she wanted to gift the pumpkins to Tobias, but she also didn't want to offend him by refusing his payment. She nodded wordlessly, taking the money from him. She counted the bills, noting it was an ample amount for a few pumpkins. She wasn't even sure how many were in his wheelbarrow. She surmised he was honest, especially since he'd been adamant about paying for them.

“Is it enough?” he inquired, studying her face intently.

“Yes, thank you,” she replied, her smile broadening.

“You have a nice day, then.” He tilted his hat, turning and heading back towards his pumpkin cart.

“You too!” Tilly called out, waving from the front door. Tobias threw his hand up in response. She observed as he wheeled his cart down the dirt lane, her eyes glued to the window pane, long after he'd disappeared down the country road.

“Who was that?” Caleb asked, stealing her attention.

Tilly stiffened, ripping her gaze away from the window. "Tobias, he stopped by to pay for the pumpkins."

Amber liquid sloshed in the glass Caleb was holding, as he took a long swig of his brew. "Man, I make some amazing sweet tea."

"Did you use Mama's recipe?" Tilly grinned.

"You bet," Caleb smirked, chuckling as he watched his sister sprint into the kitchen to pour herself a glass. He admired her spunk, and he hoped she held on to it. Life had been hard for them all, but Tilly had suffered the most. She felt things deeper than anyone he'd ever known. His sister, she was something special, and he secretly hoped she found someone who truly cherished her for the treasure she was.

## Chapter Seventeen

Since her spontaneous encounter with Tobias Gable that day on the farm, Tilly couldn't dispel him from her mind. At church the following Sunday, he sat at the antique piano, playing a flawless rendition of Amazing Grace. Hattie Mayo – their usual piano player – had been hospitalized for pneumonia, and it also didn't help that she was eighty-seven. Tilly found her eyes gravitating to the handsome fellow multiple times during service. Trina had immediately noticed her eying their pastor's nephew.

"Tilly, are you paying attention to the reverend at all?" Trina whispered harshly against her ear.

Tilly stiffened, diverting her gaze to the platform where, Reverend Vann, was preaching about the Fruits of the Spirit. Tobias had remained at the piano while the reverend taught, oblivious to the teen girl gazing dreamily at him on the middle row.

When the service had ended and the adjourning prayer was said, Tilly abruptly tore out of the chapel – her body slick with sweat despite the cool, autumn day. Caleb had stayed inside to allow Nadine and Theresa time to socialize with their friends. However, Trina, had followed after Tilly, grinning from ear to ear. Tilly had sneaked off behind the church, flinching when she heard the sound of leaves crunching behind her.

“You're sweet on the reverend's nephew, aren't you? I saw the way you were looking at him all through service. You couldn't take your eyes off of him.” Trina placed her hands on her hips, smirking, as if she'd learned the most valuable secret in the world.

Tilly flushed a deep crimson. There was no use in denying the truth because Trina was relentless when it came to confiscating information out of people.

Tilly shrugged nonchalantly. “Yeah, he's handsome. He bought some pumpkins from us last week. You can't blame a girl for lookin'.”

Trina grabbed her arm, dragging her back to the front of the church. “You should go talk to him. You're single and available, and he'll never know it if you purposely choose to remain invisible."

Before, Tilly, could object, she found herself standing face to face with Tobias. He was chatting with her brother, Caleb. "Caleb, what are our afternoon plans?" Trina interrupted, smiling sweetly. Tilly didn't like where this was going - no, not one bit.

"Well, aren't you making lunch this afternoon?" he inquired, clueless as to what she was plotting.

"Ahh, yes, you're right! Silly me, must have slipped my mind," Trina chortled, lightly touching Caleb's shoulder. Tilly kept her gaze averted, her cheeks ripening with fresh color, as Trina prattled on. "Why don't we invite Tobias? I'm sure it's been awhile since he's had a nice, home cooked meal," Trina suggested, peering at Tobias - anticipating his response.

"You have any afternoon plans, Tobias?" Caleb inquired.

Tobias blinked curiously, oblivious to what was transpiring. "No, a home cooked meal sounds grand. You sure I won't be interrupting anything?" he asked in his heart-melting southern drawl.

"Not at all," Trina affirmed.

Tilly ducked her head sheepishly, realizing she was in for a long and unpredictable afternoon.

## Chapter Eighteen

Once Caleb had began going to church, Bart Matthews had been furious, but he'd stood his ground and forced their father to allow him and his brothers to have Sundays off. There was no sense in a man working himself to death. The elder Mathews' brothers hadn't darkened a church door since they'd been granted a solitary day off through the week, but they'd stood behind Caleb when he'd confronted their father.

Sunday dinners at Trina's had become a tradition ever since. Sometimes it was just the two of them, but often times her parents joined them, or Tilly and the younger Matthews' sisters. Today someone new shared their table – Tobias Gable.

Caleb had heard through the grapevine he was 25 and originated from the hills of West Virginia. He was friendly enough but rather standoffish. Caleb wondered if there was something he was hiding, and he hadn't merely came all this way just to attend to his ill uncle. It wasn't any of his business to pry, but Caleb noticed when the table was set and they'd held hands to pray, Tilly appeared feverish when she had to hold Tobias's hand. He'd seated himself right next to her, but Caleb thought nothing of their seating arrangement. Nadine and Theresa had ventured into town with Trina's folks. There had been a promise of ice cream and a new toy. It was a good thing because Trina's dining room table only sat four. Caleb suspected, Trina had been the one to send his younger siblings off with her parents. He had a feeling she was plotting something behind his back, and seeing Tobias sitting next to Tilly made him uneasy. He noted how Tobias would sneak glances at her. Once she'd caught him looking at her, she'd quickly averted her gaze, blushing profusely. Caleb would have liked to have known what was transpiring between Tobias and his younger sister. A fierce, brotherly sense of protectiveness overwhelmed him, and he suddenly desired for Tobias Gable to disappear.

Caleb had planned on swooping in and asking him to assist him with mending, Trina's, dad’s barn door, but it was if his fiancé had read his mind because she'd requested him to help her do the dishes after lunch.

Trina had insisted, Tilly, give Tobias a tour of the place before Caleb could voice his objection. Tilly had reluctantly complied, demurely leading Tobias out the door. Caleb peered through the kitchen window, his hands plunged in soapy water, observing the pair walk towards the duck pond. His cheeks flamed as Tobias pointed towards the pond, causing his sister to bow over with laughter. His baby sister had never shown any interest in a boy, and Caleb didn't like it. It was too soon. He clenched his eyes shut, reminding himself it was merely a harmless friendship. He silently assured himself nothing would come of it as Trina hummed an old hymn to herself. He tore his gaze from the window, desiring to see no more. Pa would blow a gasket if he knew Tilly was hanging out with any boy. He was very protective of his daughters. Caleb bit his lip, hard, reminding himself he couldn't be that person. His sister was technically adult and deserved all the happiness in the world. Tobias Gable better learn his place, though. If they turned out to be more than friends, Tobias better never break her heart or he would break his face.

“Why are you staring' a hole through the window, Caleb?” Trina tilted her head to the side as she scrubbed the grease off of a soiled pan.

Caleb smirked, splashing water in her direction. Trina squealed - water drenching the front of her periwinkle, cotton dress. “Caleb Matthews! What did you do that for!?” She scowled, wrenching a wooden spoon from the dish drainer.

Caleb backed away, holding his hands up in mock surrender. “Consider that pay back for deciding to play matchmaker!”

Trina tucked the wooden spoon at her side. “What ever do you mean?” She feigned ignorance.

“Playing the fool isn't going to work on me, Trina. I've figured out your little ploy. You set this dinner up, had your parents take Nadine and Theresa into town with them, so they wouldn't be a distraction when you decided to get Tobias and my sister alone.” Caleb shot Trina an accusing glance, his right brow furrowed at her attempt to be subtle.

“Fine! You're right. I did it because I knew Tilly liked him, and she's never shown an interest in the boys we go to school with. Can you blame me for desiring a bit of happiness for my best friend?” Trina sniffled, and Caleb could tell she was on the verge of tears. Caleb gathered her hands in his own, tucking an errant strawberry curl behind her ear. Her lower lip quivered, he gently brushed his thumb across it, and she shuddered.

"I wasn't trying to be crass, sweetheart, I just don't want to see Tilly get hurt. I feel like she's actually gotten to the point where she can be carefree again, and I don't want to see somebody destroy her happiness. I don't think her heart could survive another brutal break. Losing Ma changed her, and I don't want to see her fall apart that way again," he confessed, leaning his forehead against Trina's.

Trina shook her head, gazing deeply into his eyes. "I have a good feeling about this one."

Caleb half-smiled. "You better be right, I'd hate to have to rearrange his face."

Trina punched his arm playfully. He seized her wrists, pulling her close. His breath ghosted against her lips before he captured them in a gentle kiss. She melted into his warm embrace, and when he broke the kiss, he slow danced with her in the kitchen, imagining her adorned in a white wedding gown. Soon she would take his last name, and he'd hold on to her forever. He wouldn't dream of releasing her from his grasp – his precious girl.

## Chapter Nineteen

Tilly had half the mind to crawl across the table and choke her best friend when she suggested she and Tobias take a stroll around the property. Why couldn't her 'best friend' give him a tour? It was her house for goodness sake! She felt her vexation melt away when someone gently tapped her on the shoulder. She turned on cue, meeting rich sable eyes – rendering her breathless.

“So how about that tour, Ms. Tilly?” Tobias stated invitingly.

“Sure.” She complied, pushing her chair away from the dinner table. She walked ahead of Tobias, her heart thrumming loudly in her ears – blocking out any other sound.

They halted in front of the duck pond. Tobias whistled, breaking the barrier of silence which had formed between them.

"I fell into a pond just like this when I was seven. Our old bull got loose and chased me right into the water. I loathed that animal; I'm thankful my Pa shot him afterward. Best meat I ever had."

Images of Tobias being chased by an ornery, old bull filled her head, and she gasped, peals of laughter erupting from her mouth as she bowled over. She laughed until her sides ached, and she struggled to breathe. "I'm sorry, but that was hilarious!" She continued to chuckle.

Tobias grinned. "You have a lovely smile, Tilly Matthews."

Tilly's eyes widened at the compliment, her cheeks blazing with heat. She found herself blushing more around Tobias than anyone she'd ever met. "T-Thank you," she stammered.

Tobias shoved his hands in his pockets. "My uncle wants me to drive the pickup and pull the trailer for the hayride. I was wondering if you'd like to accompany me to the church's fall festival? You could sit with me up in the cab," he asked, praying she said yes.

"I'd love to," she blurted out abruptly, without giving the invitation a second thought.

"So, it's a date, then?" he added, standing a few feet in front of her.

"It's a date," she affirmed, rocking back and forth on her heels, hands clasped demurely behind her back.

He smiled once more, flashing a row of slightly crooked, bottom teeth. "I look forward to it, I hate to run, but I better get home and check on Uncle Vann," he said, stepping forward. "I'll see you this weekend, do you care if I pick you up at your house before the festival?" he remarked casually.

Tilly's face paled as she imagined how her brothers and father would react if they witnessed a guy picking her up. "How about I just meet you at the church?" she stammered, swallowing the ball of nerves settled in her throat.

Tobias appeared crestfallen from the refusal, but he quickly straightened up, nodding. "I'll see you there, good day to you, Matilda," he addressed her formally. She cringed inwardly at his use of her full moniker, as she watched him saunter away. She hoped he didn't feel dejected because she didn't want him to pick her up at her place.

"Goodbye, Tobias!" she called back, waving. She straightened her posture. She would make him understand somehow. She had hope they would truly get to know each other. It would take time, but all good things did.

## Chapter Twenty

Tilly greeted the following weekend with exuberant anticipation. It had been difficult to keep her mind on her studies and her chores, with her date with Tobias looming in the coming days. Tilly wore her best, casual attire – a dark orange skirt, accompanied by a white sweater. Caleb and Trina had driven to the church, and she'd rode with them. Her chestnut curls cascaded down her backside in elegant waves. When Tobias had caught sight of her, her waterfall curls reflected auburn – a spectacular illusion produced by the setting sun.

When she was alone, he'd approached her, greeting her with a smile. “I'm glad you made it,” he said, hands poised at his sides.

“Where else would I be?” She smiled sheepishly, twisting

a ringlet with her index finger nervously.

Tobias shrugged. “I wasn't sure if you desired my company or not.”

Tilly shook her head. “I've been anticipating this festival all week, seeing you especially,” she confessed – the apples of her cheeks exuding a warm glow.

His muscles relaxed in relief. He offered her his arm. “Would you like to meander about? See what all they've got set up around back?”

Tilly nodded. “I'd love, too,” she said, looping her arm through his.

The first activity they came upon was apple bobbing. Several people with damp hair chuckled gaily as they walked away from the horse trough – filled with crisp, red apples.

“Are you any good?” Tobias inquired, eying her curiously.

“I'm decent,” she winked, pulling her hair back before plunging her head in the water. She emerged with a juicy red apple protruding from her mouth. Tobias chuckled, clapping in applause as she took a generous bite out of the fruit. Water dribbled down her chin, and she gratefully took the handkerchief he produced from his shirt pocket. She dabbed the water from her face, handing him the bitten apple. He took a bite from the opposite end.

Tilly frowned. “I didn't give you permission to eat my apple! Get your own!” she giggled, snatching the fruit from his hand.

Tobias covered his chest with his right hand, feigning shock. “Tilly Matthews, I'm offended! Hasn't anyone ever taught you the unwritten commandment?”

She wrinkled her nose in response. “Unwritten commandment?”

“Yes, thou shalt share your food with your friends,” he smirked, grabbing the apple out of her hand and tossing it over his shoulder. It landed near an oak, rolling into the woods behind the church.

“We're definitely not friends! I worked hard to get that apple!” She grimaced, perching a hand on her petite hip, frowning.

Tobias held up his pointer finger, sauntering towards the trough, before ducking his entire head in. Tilly clasped her hands over her mouth, gasping when he emerged with twin apples dangling from his mouth. He tossed one to her, shaking out his drenched mop of dark hair.

“You'll catch a cold! There should be a towel around here

somewhere," she remarked, hurrying towards the direction of the fellowship hall. She returned moments later, a ratty dishtowel in hand.

"Sorry, but it's all I could find," she remarked apologetically, handing him the faded piece of floral material.

"Thank you," he replied, taking the towel and squeezing out his damp curls.

Tilly shifted the apple he'd gifted her with between hands. "Can you juggle?" she inquired curiously.

"I know I'm a bit goofy, but do I look like I ran away from the circus?" he teased.

Tilly grinned. "Perhaps," she added, tossing him her apple.

He caught it, effortlessly shifting both apples between opposite hands. Tilly reached into the trough, procuring another apple and throwing it into the middle of the pair he'd been previously juggling. He managed to alternate them without any struggle, until she added a fourth to the mix. The trio of apples tumbled to the ground, followed by the fourth.

"I suppose three is all I can manage," he shrugged, bending down to retrieve them.

"I thought you did well, but I don't believe you'd make it in the circus, considering they're required to juggle swords and flaming hoops," she remarked, brushing past him.

He quickly caught up with her. "What makes you believe they juggle flaming hoops or swords?"

"My neighbors went to the circus once, they claimed an Arabian man juggled six swords and lit some hoops on fire and juggled those, too. They said it was miraculous because he didn't once get burned," she told him.

"It was probably an illusion, then. If you touch fire, it's inevitable, you're going to get burned," he added, reaching for her hand. It slipped cozily into hers, as if it had belonged there all along.

"Would you accompany me inside for some refreshments? I'm rather tired of apples," he said, his eyes twinkling with merriment.

"I'd be obliged," she returned, grinning from ear to ear. She felt at ease with the man beside her, and giddy. Tobias Gable made her feel a million sensations at once, and she was certain no one was capable of such a feat.

## Chapter Twenty-One

Tobias was an exemplary gentleman. He offered to make a plate for her and even insisted on pulling her chair out for her before she sat at the table. He'd retrieved a bowl of chili for them, a slice of Mable Green's county fair famous, pumpkin pie, and an apple fritter.

He seated himself in front of her, handing her a glass of sweet tea to wash it all down with. “So, do you like to cook?” he asked, nibbling on his apple fritter.

Tilly blew on her spoonful of chili, slowly bringing it to her mouth - relishing the way the spices minced on her tongue.

"Yes, I cook for my entire family, usually every day."

A hint of a smile bloomed to Tobias's lips, his gaze afar off when he spoke. "My mother used to cook the most spectacular apple cobbler, this fritter reminds me of her bustling around the kitchen – the scent of warm apples, soaked in brown sugar permeating the atmosphere."

"Does she still make it?" she asked daringly, an image of her own sweet mother conjuring within her subconscious.

Tobias shook his head. "The cancer got her about three years ago," he added, shifting his gaze to the half-empty plate in front of him.

"I lost my mother six years ago," she mumbled, stirring her chili absentmindedly – a subtle attempt to deflect away from her melancholy.

He must have heard her because he'd suddenly reached across the table, resting his hand atop hers. "I'm truly sorry to hear that," he remarked somberly.

"Same to you," she replied, smiling faintly.

They sat in companionable silence for a brief period, his hand never straying from hers. She wasn't sure if hours or minutes had passed when, Reverend Vann, abruptly entered the fellowship hall.

"Tobias, everyone's ready to go on the hayride," he remarked, resting his weathered hand on his nephew's shoulder.

"I'll be along in a minute," Tobias answered, severing eye contact with her.

"Alright, Tilly, will you be accompanying us on the hayride?" the reverend queried, transfixing his gaze on her.

"Of course, how are you feeling, Reverend?" Tilly inquired, silently missing the weight of Tobias's palm atop hers.

"Better – I have good and bad days," he replied, making Tilly realize his color had returned. He exhibited a healthy glow, and she hoped he was finally on the mend.

"Well, I'll be on my way out, don't keep the church folk waiting too much longer, Tobias." Reverend Vann chuckled, casting a knowing glance between them.

Tilly blushed deeply at his retort, averting her gaze to her half-empty glass of sweet tea. She studied the murky brown water intently, doing her best not to meet the gentleman's handsome face in front of her.

"Will you still be accompanying me on the hayride, Ms. Matthews?" he asked, batting his eyelashes playfully at her.

She pushed back her timidity, standing to her feet. "I'd be

obliged, Mr. Gable," she replied, proffering her hand.

The moment their fingers intertwined, Tilly felt pleasant warmth pool in her belly. Tobias led her out of the fellowship hall and into the fading light of the setting sun. When Tobias opened the passenger side door of his truck for her, she was unaware of the multiple pairs of eyes glued on them, seated in the adjoining trailer filled with straw. All she saw was him – a man she yearned to unravel layer by layer, until she possessed all of his secrets.

## Chapter Twenty-Two

Caleb observed his younger sister disappear into Tobias Gable's truck, giggling girlishly at something he'd said. Trina had told him he better lighten up. Tilly deserved happiness of her own – the kind he and Trina shared. He knew it was true, so he was doing his best to keep his temper in check. He tucked his arm around Trina's waist as the trailer began to move. She laid her head on his shoulder.

"Romantic, isn't it?" she added, gazing up at him.

"If it was just us, and this hay wagon wasn't full of people, I'd kiss you right now," he whispered against the shell of her ear.

Trina's cheeks glowed from his admission. "Caleb Matthews, we're at a church function!" she hissed under her breath, jabbing him hard in the ribs.

Caleb chuckled, kissing her temple. “None of them are paying any attention to us. Besides, you can hardly hear anything over the sound of those youngins' screaming. Must all be hyped up on sugar.”

Trina nodded, interlacing their fingers, silently praying Tilly made a personal connection with the man she was spending time with this evening.

Tobias steered the truck down several back roads. Tilly could hear the muffled conversations of the people in the trailer behind them, minced with the sounds of children laughing and cheering. His eyes were trained on the road, and a lump had settled in her throat. The ease of conversation they'd shared earlier had flitted away. Tilly closed her eyes, 'Lord, give me strength,' she prayed. She averted her gaze towards him, noting a patch of stubble on his cheek he'd missed shaving. She focused on it for a few fleeting seconds, summoning the courage to speak. “So, how long do you plan on staying in the area?” she asked, hoping his sudden arrival wasn't temporary.

Tobias rounded a curve, keeping one hand on the steering wheel while scrubbing the other down his face. She felt like she'd hit a nerve when he didn't immediately answer, but great relief flooded her chest when he abandoned his silence.

"At first, I was only going to stay a few months until Uncle recovered.  However, I don't really have a lot to go home to.  My folks have already passed.  I have an older sister that lives in Kentucky – ran away with a man my parents didn't approve of, and I haven't spoken to her since.  Uncle Vann is really the only family I have left, and I like it here.  The people are genuine, and they tend to stick together whenever there's a crisis.  That's a rare find in the world these days.  Besides, there's a pretty girl sitting next to me I'm growing quite fond of, and I'd rather stick around and get to know her better.  You never know what's just around the bend," he winked.

Pleasant warmth bubbled in her chest, seeping all the way down to her toes.  Tobias Gable was *fond* of her.  She gripped the edge of the truck seat until her fingers were bone white, afraid if she loosened her grasp that she'd float away, star struck from his confession.  The warmth curled around her being when he reached over, found her hand and held it tightly.  Too tongue tied to speak, she opted to squeeze his hand.  He did the same, and they sat in comfortable silence for the remainder of the hayride.  When they arrived back at the church, and he'd parked the truck, they lingered together for a few more moments.

"Tilly, If you're willing, I'd love for you to sit with me during service tomorrow," he stated invitingly.

"Tobias, you don't have to ask me twice," she gazed up at him, a shy smile playing upon her lips.

He felt his heart rate increase from the way she looked at him. It had been a long time since... No, he wouldn't allow his mind to gravitate to the dark recesses of his mind. The past was the past, and he couldn't change it, but he prayed for the ability to create a better future for himself. Hopefully it entailed a doe eyed, Southern belle, he couldn't seem to dispel from his mind Perhaps she was the reason God had ordained him to move here all along. Only time would tell, and today it wasn't granting him any of its secrets.

## Chapter Twenty-Three

Tobias tossed and turned all night long, groaning and moaning in his sleep, as he dreamed of billowing, black smoke and fires consuming a white farm house in the distance. It had been ages since he'd dreamed of that fateful day. He'd been powerless to prevent it, and he cried out in his sleep as he raced towards the house, but it was too late. He was always too late. He watched it combust into flames, awakening the moment the roof caved in. His eyes burst open, greeted by pale moonlight shining through the window. He blinked rapidly, noting he was soaked in sweat. He slipped out of bed, padding across the hardwood floor towards the kitchen. He was stunned to see the light already on – a beacon of hope for his cluttered mind. He walked into to the kitchen to find his uncle, nursing a cup of coffee.

"Why are you up so early, Uncle?" Tobias inquired, opening the refrigerator to grab a pitcher of ice water.

Vann shrugged. "Insomnia is the culprit, I suppose. Why are you up? You usually can sleep through anything."

"Just a bad dream, no big deal," Tobias replied, pulling out a chair and sitting across from him.

"You sure you don't want to discuss it?" the reverend inquired, his eyes swimming with concern.

Tobias waved his hand in dismissal. "No, I'm fine," he replied, deciding not to weigh him down any further with his burdens. He was finally recovering from his series of ailments, and Tobias wouldn't risk causing him to relapse. They'd both suffered from severe losses, but there was no point in contending with the past. It couldn't be changed.

"You're a terrible liar, but I'm not going to pry. I think I'll try and get a few more hours of shuteye before the sun rises. I hope you'll do the same," Vann replied, leaving the table. He clasped his shoulder affectionately as he passed him.

Tobias stared at the water, sitting motionless in his glass – hoping to draw his attention away from the storm brewing within his mind. Unlike his uncle, he didn't return to bed that night. He was too afraid of reliving the haunting images which had assaulted his dreams. Instead, he'd pulled out his Holy Bible, poring over the Psalms until he felt peace return to his heart and mind. He sensed the Holy Spirit ministering to him as he continued to read through his Bible, especially the portion about Jesus promising to give him peace which passes understanding. Jesus had been his peace through these last oppressive years. Clinging to his Savior had been the only thing which had kept him from losing his mind. He clearly remembered the night God had awoken him and told him to go and live with his uncle – a man he'd only visited a handful of times during his life. Tobias had packed up his few belongings the next day, and driven over two hundred miles to his residence.

“I've been expecting you, The Lord told me you were coming,” Vann had informed him the moment he answered the door. He hadn't moved here to care for his ailing relative; he'd moved because God had commanded him to. Of course, Tobias had used his Uncle's illnesses as his primary reason for the move, whenever someone inquired as to why he'd ventured so far. It hadn't been a lie; he believed it was one reason God had told him to come here. His uncle needed help with mundane tasks since he'd fallen ill. He was certain it was one of God's intentions for asking him to move in with the reverend. However, he believed his move entailed more than just what he could see and feel at this present moment. He felt like there was something looming just over the horizon for him, something he wasn't anticipating. But it would be exactly what he needed, and what he'd been praying for.

## Chapter Twenty-Four

Tilly gathered eggs from the chicken coop early Sunday morning. It's what her father had demanded her to do. She wasn't thrilled he'd stumbled into her bedroom at 4:00 A.M., cussing and rambling nonsense about her not pulling her weight around the farm. The instant she'd smelled the whiskey on his breath, she knew there was no trifling with him. She was just grateful he hadn't disturbed the girls. Seeing him in his drunken and disoriented state wasn't how she wanted him to be presented to her sisters. She'd hoped he would become a better man for them, but his drunkenness had only increased throughout the years. If it hadn't been for Caleb, Thomas, and Beau, the farm would've gone under years ago. She feared one morning she'd find him dead, lying in a pool of his own vomit.

Many a night, she soaked her pillow through with tears, praying her daddy's heart would turn back to the God which loved him with reckless abandon.

However, she often felt her prayers didn't make it past the ceiling because she hadn't witnessed a visible change in him after all these years. Despite his willingness to surrender his heart to God, Tilly continued being faithful to her maker. She could barely keep her eyes open when they pulled up to church that morning, but she had determined not to miss. Her eyes burned and blurred as she made it into the church. She scanned the sanctuary for Tobias, spotting him on the second row from the front. She proceeded to his pew, halting a few times to shake hands and greet other members of their congregation. She'd told Trina about Tobias inviting her to sit with him. Trina had grinned from ear to ear, promising to encourage her younger sisters to stay with her and Caleb, during the service. Tilly was grateful for her friend's support. She didn't need two curious girls to pepper her with questions. They'd been too busy with festival games the previous night to inquire about her sister's handsome 'friend'. Tilly commanded her heartbeat to settle as she sat beside the gentleman which had called her pretty mere hours ago. Flushing at the memory, she silently took her place beside him. He'd been staring silently at the pulpit, his mind in a faraway place, she assumed.

"Good morning, Tobias," she greeted him, pulling him from his reverie.

Tobias startled, meeting her gaze. "Oh, hey there, Tilly. I'm ashamed to say that I didn't even notice you had sat down. I didn't sleep hardly any last night, so my mind is a bit fuzzy. You'll have to excuse me," he replied, placing his hand over his mouth to stifle back a yawn.

"No worries, I didn't sleep all that soundly myself," she added, jarred by the memory of her father forcing her to get out of bed earlier that morning – drunk as a skunk.

"We're in the same boat, it seems. Hopefully my uncle won't lull us to sleep this Sunday. I hope he has a fiery sermon prepared for us. The Holy Spirit is really going to have to shake me awake this morning," he chuckled, slipping his hand into hers.

Tilly chortled at his response. "God knows what we need when we need it. I'm sure he has us both in mind this morning," she responded, squeezing his hand gently.

He nodded, granting her an affirming smile as Owen Cantrell – their church elder – opened the service with prayer.

Tilly slipped her hand up when Owen asked if anyone had any unspoken prayer requests. Tears pricked at her eyes as she recounted her father's state of disarray that morning. Her heart was laden with the lost state of his soul. She hadn't wanted to make her request public because Caleb would have interrogated her about it after service. She hadn't mentioned the incident which had happened between them because she knew Caleb would have gone stark, raving mad. He loathed their father's drinking as much as she did, but he wasn't usually as forgiving. He would argue with their dad during his drunken state. One time, Caleb had even chased him off the farm when he'd threatened to burn the house down while they were still in it. Caleb, nor her other brothers barely acknowledged him unless it was business related. Tilly desperately tried to have a relationship with him when he was sober. He wasn't a mean man, but he was a cruel drunk. He hadn't always been, but the alcohol had warped his personality, transforming him into an unrecognizable monster whenever he'd had too much to drink. When he drank beer, he was tolerable – sometimes even friendly, but the whiskey made him unbearable. She remembered a time when Beau had poured all of his liquor down the drain. Bart Matthews had been furious, and probably would have killed his own son if Caleb and Thomas hadn't intervened.

As much as she loved her father, Tilly vowed to never marry a man like him. Her eyes gravitated to Tobias as he sat behind the piano. His deep baritone drifted throughout the room as he serenaded them with a classic hymn, “Nothing but the Blood of Jesus”. Tilly wasn't sure if the charming, Tobias Gable, was the man she was meant to make a life with, but if he was, she prayed God would remind them to keep Him at the center of their relationship because without Him, Tilly knew her life would be in complete shambles, as it once was. However, because of the blood Jesus shed for her, it was possible for her to have an abundant life – the exact one he'd designed just for her.

## Chapter Twenty-Five

Fall gave away to winter, and soon snow blanketed the rolling hills in all its white glory. Tilly pulled her toboggan over her ears, her cheeks turned ruddy from the bitter cold. She'd been feeding the hogs when she felt something wet and chilled hit her on the side of the head. She pivoted on her heel, immediately spying Tobias, standing close by. He tossed another snowball between both of his gloved hands, snickering as he hurled it in her direction. She effortlessly dodged it, evading his attack.

"What are you doing here?" she scowled, perching a hand on her elegant hip.

"Now, is that any way to treat your boyfriend?" He placed his hand over his heart, feigning shock.

Tilly guffawed at his antics, bounding towards him. He

opened his arms as she jumped into his awaiting embrace. "You know I'm always happy to see you, you goof!" She pulled his cap down over his eyes in retaliation. He grinned – pulling his hat off, kissing her brow affectionately. Dark raven curls masked his eyes. She reached up to brush them aside. They stayed still for a few brief seconds, gazing ardently into each others' eyes. The moment ceased when several snowballs pummeled them at once. They disengaged, jumping apart to spy two giggling girls throwing multiple snowballs at them.

"Get 'em, girls!" Caleb hollered. He stood behind them, egging them on.

Tilly chuckled, brushing the snow from her cardigan. She bent over, packing snow in her gloved hands. She glanced over, observing Tobias mimicking her actions. He grinned at her before he threw the snowball. It slammed right into Caleb's nose. He staggered backwards, resulting in Nadine and Theresa, bursting into a fit of giggles. Caleb quickly recovered from Tobias's assault. He jumped to his feet, launching a counter attack at Tilly's boyfriend. Tilly had thrown her snowball at her sisters; it had landed in a heap on the ground. She'd soon joined them, observing her older brother and boyfriend, engaging in a snowball fight. The three girls cheered simultaneously when Caleb surrendered. It turned out, Tobias was the master of all snowball fights.

Tilly couldn't suppress her growing smile as Caleb slapped Tobias on the back in a brotherly gesture. At first, Caleb's demeanor had been glacial towards him. He hadn't been open about them being together, but Tobias had gradually won him over – with his “good ole' boy” persona. They'd been courting for two months, and Tilly couldn't have been happier.

Tobias was different from all the local boys Tilly had grown up with. He was mannerly and filled with Biblical knowledge, which they conversed about often. Reverend Vann had been ill for a couple of Sundays, and Tobias had taken charge – leading the congregation in worship and prayer. He'd even preached a sermon. It had been about Jabez – a man from the Old Testament. There wasn't much known about him, except for a few scriptures found in 1 Chronicles, chapter four. He'd taught on the portion where, Jabez, had asked God to enlarge his territory. He'd told the congregation it was their responsibility as Christians to ask God for more spiritual territory, so his heavenly kingdom might flourish throughout the earth – shining his glory on mankind at all corners of the world. Tilly was too busy daydreaming about her boyfriend, to notice

Theresa had wandered towards the frozen cow pond.

A shrill scream pervaded the air. Caleb and Tobias instinctively turned, gazing briefly at each other before dashing off in the direction of the frozen pond. Theresa flailed her arms, shrieking frightfully as she sputtered helplessly. Caleb dove right into the icy breach, hauling Theresa to the surface. Tilly held Nadine close as she watched her boyfriend pull them both out of the frigid water.

"Tilly, get Nadine inside and get a fire going. We need to get them warmed up!" Tobias commanded.

"I'm fine!" Caleb retorted gruffly – teeth chattering, as he held his shivering six year old sister in his arms.

Tilly grabbed Nadine's hand, running up the icy steps and into the house. The old wood stove was still burning, permeating the kitchen with heat. It only needed a few logs added to the fire. Tilly stoked the flames with a metal poker as Caleb hauled Theresa into the house.

"Nadine, go upstairs and get her some dry clothes," Tilly commanded as Caleb sat her in front of the stove. He shed his drenched jacket by the door before heading upstairs to change. Tobias appeared a few moments later with an armful of wood.

"Thank you," Tilly replied gratefully as he emptied them

into the stove's chamber.

Nadine appeared seconds later, carrying a long sleeved night dress and stockings. Tobias wordlessly went upstairs to check on Caleb as Tilly stripped away her sister's wet things. She squeezed out Theresa's drenched hair, pulling the gown over her head. Nadine lightly scolded her when Theresa began to fuss about Tilly telling her she had to wear her stockings.

"It's up to bed with you, Theresa. I'll call, Doc Jacobs and have him come and examine you, but you need to stay warm-"

Tilly halted when she heard a booming voice echo throughout the room. "What's all this about!? Why are there wet clothes all over the floor!?" Bart Matthews chided, appearing in the doorway.

Tilly felt the color drain from her face as she turned to see their father, shielding Nadine and Theresa from his fury. "Theresa thought she could step on the ice on the cow pond, but it was thin, and she fell through. Caleb jumped in and saved her; Tobias helped," she stammered.

Bart narrowed his gaze, glaring daggers at her. He strode towards her, grabbing her shirt collar. He lifted her up, choking the air from her lungs as he held her by the throat. She could smell the whiskey on his breath. During the dead of winter, he still drank. Fear invaded her entire being, and she felt like she was staring the devil right in the eyes. The echo of her sisters' cries didn't register in her ears, nor the stampede of footsteps coming down the stairs. She gasped for breath as she fell to the ground in a heap. Caleb had tackled Bart to the ground, and Tobias had managed to find some twine and restrained his wrists. Bart cursed and kicked as the boys threw him in the linen closet and shut the door. Caleb tended to Nadine and Theresa, which were sobbing uncontrollably. Spots of color blurred Tilly's vision as Tobias settled onto the floor, gathering her into his consoling embrace.

"Let me see," he crooned, pulling down her turtleneck, spying her father's angry hand print.

"It'll probably bruise, let's put a cool cloth on it," he added, helping her into a chair. She instantly missed his body heat. She laid her head down as he soaked a dish towel under the faucet.

"You never told me father your drank or had violent episodes," Tobias remarked quietly, pressing the cool cloth against the abrasion forming on her neck.

Tilly winced, turning her head to the side. "I didn't want to worry you, and besides, we've not been together that long," she remarked coolly.

Tobias stiffened at her retort, hurt flashing in his sable depths. “You're right, but I...no, never mind, it's not important.” He left the damp cloth draped around her neck. “I'll head on up the road and tell the Jacobs' what happened, and then I'll be on my way,” he responded without meeting her gaze.

Guilt coiled around her chest as she watched him leave without saying a word. They'd never fought like this before, only the usual playful banter couples typically shared, but his words held a deeper meaning. He was concealing something. Tilly didn't have time to mull over it before the Jacobs had came bursting through the door. Mrs. Jacobs fussed over Tilly's bruises and made a pot of hot tea for them all. Mr. Jacobs had examined them all before calling the cops and filing a police report. Tilly's heart clenched painfully as she watched two policemen escort her father away, but he'd more than proven he was a danger to them all. The realization he'd nearly killed her sank in, once the shock had cleared. As she laid in bed that night, huddled between her sisters, who were keen about keeping her at arm's length – she knew she owed Tobias a deep, heartfelt apology. She swore to herself there would no more secrets between them, for she was ready to lay her heart bare before him.

## Chapter Twenty-Six

Nadine and Theresa had opted to be quiet at breakfast that morning. They'd witnessed the one thing she'd tried so desperately to shield them from – their father's unyielding anger. She'd woken up and coerced Theresa into the bath. Nadine had insisted on helping, refusing to leave her side. It was imperative they discuss what had transpired, though she wasn't sure a six and seven year old would fully comprehend the words alcoholism and addiction. Their father was a drunk, but he had rarely engaged with his younger daughters. He usually ignored them; completely forgetting they were his children. It vexed Tilly for him to treat them like they were invisible, but she supposed it had truly been a blessing in disguise, considering he'd never laid a hand on them.

After Tilly had cleared away the breakfast dishes, Mr. Jacobs had shown up at the door. He informed her he'd been down to the station and had talked with the sheriff. Bart Matthews was incarcerated and would be in holding until his court date arrived. Tilly's stomach lurched when he mentioned her having to testify about him nearly taking her life. It chilled her to the bone to think what might have happened if Tobias and Caleb hadn't intervened.

Tobias. Tilly's heart wrenched with guilt as she recounted how poorly she'd treated him. She needed to make things right, and thank him for having a hand in saving her. Before Mr. Jacobs departed, he'd reassured her Rosalie would stop by at lunchtime to check on them. The icing on top of their proverbial cake was it was only a week until Christmas. Their father would be spending it in jail, and though he was her least favorite person at the moment, she couldn't help but feel a gnawing ache within her soul.

This would be the first Christmas they'd spend without

him, despite his loathsome habits and behavior. However, this Christmas would be her first with Tobias, and Thomas and Beau both had new wives – Lydia and Ava. They weren't well acquainted because her older brothers refused to bring their brides around their deranged father. They'd rushed over that morning to check in on them, after they'd heard the news. Beau's wife – Lydia – had made a peach cobbler, and Thomas's wife – Ava – had promised to cook a hearty supper for them that evening.

Tilly had anticipated Tobias stopping by sometime during the day, but when he hadn't, she'd pleaded with Mrs. Jacobs to watch the girls for an hour. She felt a sudden urge of desperation to see him. She'd instantly agreed, though Nadine and Theresa were reluctant to allow Tilly out of their sight. Tilly promised they'd bake Christmas cookies once she returned, if they'd allow her to sneak away for an hour. Baking sweets was the perfect source of bribery because they were soon waving her out the door, reminding her when she returned, that she owed them a batch of sugar cookies.

Tobias lived with his uncle, and it was only a half a mile – or so – down the lane. She'd bundled up to her nose – her toboggan sat snugly atop her head. When she'd made it to the reverend's driveway, she spotted Tobias, shoveling snow. If he'd heard her approaching, then he seemed oblivious because he kept shoveling the walkway. She stood a stone's throw away, mustering the courage to speak.

Tilly inhaled sharply, focusing on the crisp, winter air filling her lungs. “Tobias,” she spoke his name. He halted his shoveling, transfixing his gaze on her ruddy cheeks.

They stared at each other – eternity trapped between them. Tobias broke the silence first, his eyes filled with raw, unadulterated love for her. “Tilly, we may not have been together long, but my heart would have shattered into a million pieces if I'd lost you yesterday. They might as well put me six feet under if it were to happen because losing you would utterly wreck me,” he professed, tears leaking from his eyes as he enunciated each syllable.

His declaration shook her to the core, and her resolve crumbled as he closed the distance between them, reaching up to brush stray tears from her eyes. She hadn't realized she'd been crying until he gingerly cupped her right cheek within his gloved palm.

The words she'd meant to say died on her tongue like

simmering embers, so she allowed her body to say what she couldn't. She reached up to wrap her arms around his neck. She stood on her tiptoes, kissing him without reserve, right in the middle of the driveway. The world tilted on its axis as their lips collided. This kiss was unlike any they'd shared. It was filled with scorching emotion – a deep passion which could only be felt by two people irrevocably in love. Tobias broke the kiss when his hands gained the desire to roam over her immaculate curves. They knew each other only in mind and spirit, but in time they would know each other in body, too. Although it wouldn't be until she shared his last name, and the burning desire to ask her to become his wife suddenly overwhelmed him. His heart had set itself on marrying Tilly Matthews, mere days after they'd met. However now wasn't the time or place for it. There was much they still needed to discuss, and declaring meaningful sentiments in the heat of the moment wasn't always wise. Tobias closed his eyes, willing his heartbeat to still as he leaned his forehead against hers.

"We need to talk," he respired.

"I know," she nodded amicably, "I'm sorry for shutting you out."

He shook his head, caressing her cheek lovingly. "Don't

be, let's just promise to do better from now on. It's time to move forward."

"Where would you like me to begin?" she inquired.

"From the beginning, I want to know everything about you," he coaxed gently.

"Fine, but not today. I promised the girls I would be home soon, they need me," she added, her lip quivering slightly. He traced the outline of her lips with his index finger, causing butterflies to flutter madly in her abdomen.

"Tomorrow then, and not a day later," he requested.

"I promise," she vowed, reaching up to kiss him again – a smattering of snowflakes drifted around them, signaling the birth of a love which was destined to last a lifetime.

## Chapter Twenty-Seven

Tilly's older brothers and their wives had opted to stay the night. Ava had prepared a magnificent feast for them – the exact kind Mother would've approved of. Laughter had echoed throughout the old farmhouse, late into the evening. It was a queer noise because their home hadn't seemed like a cheerful place in many years. It was as if the devil had been booted out of his terrain by the foot of Almighty God Himself. She realized her father had chosen the broad way, which led to destruction. She couldn't control him – make him turn from his wicked ways.

He had to do so on his own, by making better choices. He was at rock bottom and the only place left to look was up. She silently prayed God would meet him where he was – at his lowest point – and he would have a genuine change of heart.

The following morning, Tilly was roused from her slumber by a faint thumping at her bedroom window. Wrapping her cotton robe around her, she'd padded to the window and witnessed Tobias standing below. He beamed, tossing a snowball up in the air – the object he'd used to disturb her sleep. The first light of dawn splattered the sky in a brilliant array of pinks, oranges, and golds. It was a breathtaking phenomenon, a glorious backdrop to compliment the man standing in front of it. A man – she realized she loved deeply, since yesterday afternoon. She'd held up her index finger, signaling he give her a minute. He grinned, waving her away. She'd dressed hurriedly and quietly. As she tiptoed down the stairs, she could hear a symphony of obnoxious snuffles coming from her brothers' rooms. She silently wondered how Ava or Lydia dealt with Thomas and Beau's snoring, and in a few short months, Trina would be experiencing the same issue with Caleb. She smirked in satisfaction at the thought of Trina walloping Caleb in the head with a pillow, for keeping her awake at night. It was bound to happen. She grabbed a pen, quickly scribbling down a note about who she was with. The chilly morning air whipped her in the face as soon as she'd opened the screen door. It shut precariously behind her, exuding a loud screech.

“Tilly Mathews, isn't very discreet, now is she?” Tobias jested, tapping his chin playfully.

Tilly rolled her eyes, closing the distance between them. “And Tobias Gable doesn't comprehend that a girl needs her beauty rest,” she quipped.

His features softened as he gently reached up to cradle her face within his palms. “No amount of rest is going to have any effect on your beauty, trust me, sweetheart,” he added, utilizing the endearment for the first time.

She was rendered speechless by his prose, her heart rate significantly increasing. “So, where are you taking me – to talk,” she stammered.

“I thought we'd go to a quiet and peaceful place. The truck is already running around back,” he replied.

“Okay, I'm ready, though I'd advise you not to kiss me, I sort of forgot to brush my teeth,” she added, blushing crimson. He wrinkled his nose playfully. “What did you have for dinner last night? Onions?”

She jabbed him playfully in the ribs, smirking. “Even worse...garlic.” She blew warm, stale air in his face. She didn't take the time to register his reaction, and pranced around the house where he'd parked the truck. The engine rumbled, and she sighed in anticipation as she made her way to the passenger side. She opened the door, a wave of warm heat blowing in her face. She shivered as the door shut, crowding against the truck vents – savoring the warmth which radiated from them. Tobias slid into the driver's side seconds later.

“You really took my breath away back there,” he remarked, waving his hand in front of his face teasingly.

Peals of laughter erupted from her throat. “So, where are you taking me?”

“To the church, it's private. It just felt like the right place,” he shrugged, his tone growing serious.

“I agree,” Tilly added, clasping his hand securely in hers.

Tobias slipped off her mitten and drew her hand to his lips. He kissed the underside of her wrist reverently, sending heat pooling in her belly. “No matter what confessions are made today, I promise I'm here for the long haul. I ain't leavin',” he said in his heavy, Southern drawl.

“Me neither,” she vowed, locking gazes with the man she

grew to love more with every passing second.

When they arrived, the church was vacant. The brilliant sun beamed down on the frozen steeple; clumps of snow fell from the roof, into a heap on the ground. Tobias had aided her up the slippery steps, jamming his key into the lock and pushing open the door, which creaked with age. The sanctuary was quiet and blessedly warm. She assumed Tobias had already stopped by to turn on the furnace, ensuring it would be warm and toasty upon their arrival. Tobias pulled the door closed, locking it for their privacy. Tilly was certain they'd be the church's only visitors until Sunday morning service rolled around. She supposed he did it for his own peace of mind. She stood back a few paces as he strode towards the piano. He gesticulated for her to sit beside him on the empty bench. She swiftly followed, settling down beside him.

The atmosphere was heavy with hesitation; the only sound which could be heard was their synchronized heart beats. Tobias respired deeply, the words spilling from his mouth like an overturned ink pot onto a blank parchment. “I was married once before; It's been nearly three years since I lost my wife and son in a horrendous fire. She said she was going to lay down for a nap since the baby was already sleeping. I told her I aimed to ride into town and pick up some bread and milk from the grocer. I idled a bit, saw an old buddy of mine at the store, and I talked with him for nearly an hour; When I arrived home, the roof caved in before my very eyes, I was too late... The fire marshal claimed it was an electrical fire. To this day, I blame myself. If I'd been home, then I could have prevented it. The painful part is, I don't know if they suffered or if smoke inhalation consumed them first. I still dream of that fateful day, often. It's like the devil won't let me forget. I sense him whispering in my ear, reminding me of how much of a failure I am. I was supposed to protect them, and I..." Tobias trailed off, his body wracking with sobs.

Tilly was flummoxed by his confession – to think of having to live with such an insurmountable burden all those short years. She almost understood, but her loss seemed miniscule compared to his. She still had the support of her family and friends after her mother's tragic passing, but who did Tobias have? He'd mentioned before that his family had been deceased for several years. Who did he have left? Had he came to her quiet town to escape his pain? Her mind buzzed with questions, but instead of speaking, she held him as he fell apart. As his body quaked with sobs, she whispered quiet, crooning words within his ear.

Tilly wasn't sure if minutes or hours had passed before he dared to speak again. “Her name was Elizabeth, and she would be 26 this year.” He paused for a moment, his resolve threatening to crumble once more. “And his name was Nathaniel; he was just six months old.”

Tilly inhaled sharply, daring to break the fragile silence which hung between them. “You can say their names, it's okay. It will always be okay,” she mumbled, carding her fingers through his curls in a soothing manner.

He turned, closing his eyes while leaning his forehead against hers. “It's your turn,” he whispered brokenly.

Tilly gathered her bearings, an image of her mother's serene face filling her head. “My mother died when I was 13, of a heart attack. I was left to pick up the pieces and become the woman of the household. I had to quit school and care for my younger sisters, make sure the meals were cooked and the house was clean. I was resentful for a lot of those years, especially when Daddy started drinking. At times he was sober, but he wallowed in his pain so much, that it became impossible for him to function without the liquor. He'd often have violent outbursts, but honestly,” she paused, catching her breath, “he never attempted to hurt me until that night."

Tobias's sable eyes darkened with ire. "And he'll never lay another hand on you again, as long as I live," he pledged.

"So, does that make you my knight in shining armor, then?" She batted her eyelashes playfully to lighten their somber moods.

"I'm actually probably more along the lines of a redneck Romeo," he chuckled softly.

"Even better," she replied, interlacing their fingers. They remained at the church for several more hours, relishing each other's company and conversing about their lives. Tilly had never opened up to anyone like she had Tobias, and she knew what they had was sacred and rare; After a day of baring each others souls, she knew without a doubt, God had sent this beautiful, loving man into her life. They were each others to cherish, and she knew her mother would fully approve of their union. Deep within, she knew her longings for a husband had been answered. And she suspected within a few months she'd be saying, "I do".

## Chapter Twenty-Eight

Christmas Day finally arrived, and the Matthews' children did their best to remain cheerful. Mr. and Mrs. Jacobs had stopped by with an assortment of gifts and robust dishes. Ava had done most of the cooking, though Tilly had reassured her multiple times she was capable of making Christmas dinner for everyone. She'd been doing it for years, ever since Mother's passing. The woman with ice-blonde hair had simply waved her away, encouraging her to help her sisters' open their gifts. Everyone anticipated for the pile of gifts to be for Nadine and

Theresa, but it turned out there was a little something for everyone. Nadine and Theresa had received new dolls, accompanied by complimentary outfits, sewn by Mrs. Jacobs herself. Everyone else received Christmas tins, filled with baked goods and store gift certificates. However, there had been a small box addressed to Tilly. Tilly loosened the delicate red ribbon from around the parcel, gingerly opening it to find a dainty silver chain with a gold angel charm dangling from it. The angel had her hands clasped together in prayer. Tilly turned the charm over in awe, finding her mother's name, followed by her birth and death date inscribed on the back. Tears misted behind her eyes, as she gently clasped the chain around her neck. The angel charm rested near her heart – a reminder that her mother was always watching over her. Her family had complimented the beauty of her necklace, and she felt fiercely protective of it, even denying a crying Theresa from borrowing it. The necklace felt like something she didn't have to share with anyone. It was something all her own, and it had been years since she'd been able to be selfish about anything. Of the few personal belongings she did own, they were at the mercy of her younger sisters. Many mishaps had happened with her favorite paints and childhood toys. She'd made peace with her losses, but the necklace felt sacred. No, she wouldn't allow it out of her sight or oblige anyone else to wear it. It was significantly special, and it was all hers.

Theresa eventually ceased begging for the necklace, easily distracted by her new doll and various baubles. Tobias had picked her up later in the afternoon, and they'd gone sledding down Dewberry Hill – the tallest incline in the entire county. Tilly warmed herself by the fire after their afternoon venture. She licked her chapped lips as Tobias admired her rosy cheeks – enhanced by the firelight.

"Your necklace is lovely, Tilly, perhaps we could ask the Jacobs where they purchased it and buy your sisters one next Christmas," Tobias suggested, adding a few more logs to the hearth.

Tilly stiffened slightly. "I think they're way too young to handle something so fragile," she replied possessively. Truthfully, she didn't want her sisters to share a replica of her cherished treasure. It was a uniquely made piece, and having another like it made it feel cheap and tarnished.

"Or not," Tobias mumbled, detecting the agitation in her voice.

Tilly sighed, feeling the Holy Spirit prick her heart for

acting so miserly. If it wasn't for the Jacobs' generosity, she wouldn't have received such a splendid gift. “I'm sorry, it's just, I've never gotten a present this costly before. My entire life I've had to give and give, until it seemed I couldn't bear to consign another piece of myself, lest I vanish into nothingness.”

Tobias placed a reassuring hand on her shoulder. “And that's why I love you, you're already outwardly beautiful, but your inner beauty is just astounding. It radiates from your inner being, amplifying your outward appearance.”

She sucked in a deep breath as he knelt beside her, rendered breathless from his amorous declaration. Unbidden tears spilled over her lashes as he removed a black velvet box from his coat pocket. “I don't have any fancy speeches prepared for this occasion, though I've mulled over in my head how this could go a thousand times. I can't give you riches untold or a mansion in Beverly Hills. All I have to offer you is myself – a sinner saved by the Grace of God. I don't have many earthly possessions, but I am filled with an abounding measure of love. I can love you, Tilly Matthews, imperfect as I am. Will you bestow upon me the honor of becoming my wife?” he proposed, flicking open the box to reveal a modest diamond settled in the center of a slender gold band.

As humble as it was, in her eyes it glimmered brighter than a thousand suns. She threw her arms around his neck, sobbing into his ebony curls, overwhelmed by emotion. “Yes, I'll marry you. Wild horses couldn't keep me away,” she consented, her voice thick with emotion.

They stayed wrapped in each others arms for awhile, clinging to the hope of a new beginning. When she composed herself long enough for him to slip the ring on her third left finger, she sensed the precipice of answered longings and fulfilled desires.

He gently brushed the tears from her eyes, smiling softly. “I've had that ring since before I moved here. God prompted me to buy it before I left town. I resisted, but the nudge was so strong I had no choice but to comply. I had no idea what I'd find once I arrived, part of me thought I'd hang around for a few months and then travel on. I wasn't sure what I was searching for, but meeting you made me want to put down roots and stay forever.”

Tilly nodded amicably, recounting Starla's promise to fund her education. It was all she'd ever dreamed about for many months, but now she couldn't bear the thought of leaving. It literally pained her to even consider it. She felt the Holy Spirit whisper to her, reminding her she was right where she belonged in that moment. She felt inner peace, knowing God would utilize for artistic talents however he saw fit in the future. Somehow she knew this was the right path for her, which meant becoming Tobias's wife and continuing to care for her sisters. She realized God needed her to remain here for a season. Tilly wasn't sure if her season would last a lifetime or for just a few more years, but she was ready to embrace it. No matter what her path entailed, she knew her Heavenly Father would be with her every step of the way, preparing the road ahead before she ever traipsed upon it. The secure weight of Tobias's hand resting in hers was a consolation, a reminder not one of her prayers had ever fallen to the ground. He'd heard her heart's every plea, and today was a beautiful reminder of her God's unfailing faithfulness. Forever near her, forever hearing her.

## Chapter Twenty-Nine

When the snow had thawed, and tiny green shoots began to burst forth from the ground, Tilly found herself standing in front of a county court judge. It was the trial which would sentence her father for attempting to murder her. Bart Matthew's hung his head in shame as Tilly recited her testimony against him. He was sober but didn't deny what had happened that fateful night in December. When he answered the judge's questions, he never made eye contact with his daughter. He appeared to be near his breaking point when the judge sentenced him to ten years in prison for attempted murder. The entire Matthews' family had been present except for the younger pair. Tilly noted how her brothers greeted their father with icy glares, appearing ready to stone him if given the chance. Tilly had every right in the world to be vexed at him, but despite what he'd done to her, all she felt was pity towards him – pity for throwing away his life so carelessly. But now he would remain behind bars for years because of his careless actions. Before the judge had ordered him to be sent away, Tilly had requested to say a few more words. As she spoke, she pictured Jesus hanging on the cross, dying for all of humanity, including her destitute, earthly father.

She squared back her shoulders, transfixing her gaze on his somber green eyes. “Daddy, despite the cruelty you subjected me to, I forgive you, and I pray for your soul every night. I pray you find Jesus, and that you allow his love to fill every empty crevice in your heart. I pray when your sentence is lifted, you'll emerge a new man. Please, learn to forgive yourself and be a better man, not just for your family but for yourself as well,” she told him. He nodded wordlessly, his eyes rueful and downcast as the bailiff led him away.

Tilly arrived home, feeling hollow. She kicked off her

shoes beside the door. Heading up to her room and sleeping away the rest of this terrible day seemed as if it were the only consolation which would appease her restless mind at the moment. Instead, she found herself standing in front of her parent's bedroom door. She precariously pushed the door open; it emitted a restless creak as she stepped inside. The bed was neatly made – the room left untouched. When her mother had passed, her father couldn't bring himself to spend another night in their old room. He'd taken the girls former room for himself, forcing the sisters to share. It felt like a silent, empty tomb, as she gazed at the nightstand, coated with dust. She traced her finger across it, leaving a lopsided imprint. Tilly's eyes gravitated to the closet door. She tiptoed towards it, wrenching it open. She scanned the closet, still filled with Mother's clothes. Her eyes halted on a white box, settled on the top shelf. Tilly stood on tiptoe, reaching for the box her spirit was suddenly drawn to. The moment she touched it, she remembered everything. Images of her last day spent with her mother flashed within Tilly's mind, startling her at how vivid they were. She clumsily dropped the box. It crashed to the floor, revealing dozens of pieces of crumpled paper.

“NO! NO!” Tilly cried, attempting to piece the shattered

box back together. When she deemed her task futile, she resigned herself to leaning against the wall. She reached for one of the folded pieces, opening it.

*Please allow my Tilly to grow up to become a beautiful, God-fearing woman.*

Tilly marveled at her mother's faded handwriting in awe. She'd stumbled upon her mother's old alabaster box – her prayer box. Tears trickled down her cheeks as she reread the prayer request over and over.

"Mama, I'd like to think this prayer has been answered, though I'm still a work in progress." A watery chuckle escaped her lips as she continued to read the other prayer requests. Some were about church members, but most were about her family.

*Please allow my boys to find good, godly women to marry that won't lead them astray.*

*Let my life be an example to my children for years to come.*

*Help Tilly to discover her talents and use them for your glory.*

*Help my little darlings Nadine and Theresa grow into exemplary young women for you Lord.*

All of the prayer requests were heartfelt, and Tilly recounted how God's hand had been in all of them. Beau and Thomas both had godly wives, though they hadn't yet made the commitment to live for the Lord on their own, she sensed they weren't far from salvation's door. Caleb had made the plunge and would be marrying her best friend in a few short weeks. Nadine and Theresa both loved going to church, and she would continue to help guide them in the right direction throughout their young lives, so they would be encouraged to stay on the narrow path when they were older. She'd discovered her unquenchable love for the arts, and was utilizing her talent for God by volunteering to paint a mural in one of their church's Sunday school classrooms. It may have seemed like a waste to some, but she was doing work for the kingdom of God – no matter how insignificant others may have deemed it.

Tilly gathered up the remaining alabaster fragments, praying Tobias would be able to mend it. She noted a folded piece of paper she had missed. It only held three words, but the weight of them burdened her heart.

*Help my husband.*

A plea from her mother's heart for her prodigal husband.

Tilly closed her eyes, clenching the thin slip of paper within her fist. "Yes, Lord Jesus, please help my father to become the man you destined him to be."

Tilly wasn't sure how long she remained in the closet, poring over the requests in her mother's box which still remained unanswered. The remnants of shattered alabaster in front of her reminded her of how God had broken her, so the contents of her character would flow into the lives of others. He'd anointed the broken places in her life with his precious love, and gingerly placed them back together. The prayer requests in her mother's alabaster box symbolized the precious perfume Mary Magdalene had used to wash Jesus' feet. The box had been a priceless heirloom to Diane Matthews, but what the box contained was even more valuable.

Tilly wasn't sure if hours or minutes had passed when she emerged from her parents' room. She walked outside to see the sun setting behind the horizon – compelling her to gather her paints and easel. For the remainder of the afternoon, Tilly painted until bright stars dotted the black vast expanse of sky. She painted until her fingers grew numb and her mind was empty of color. She painted until she could rest easy that night, knowing God was in control of everything.

## Chapter Thirty

"I'm sorry how everything played out with your dad. I know you love him, but what he did was wrong and he needs to suffer the consequences," Tobias told Tilly the following day, as they sat on her front porch that afternoon.

Tilly nodded, stealing a brief glance at her future husband. "Despite everything, I still forgive him. I want him to find the peace we have, the peace only Jesus can give." A gentle breeze toussled her curls as she stared towards the horizon.

Tobias reached out to take her hand. "And that's one of

the many reasons why I adore you so much – your forgiving heart."

Tilly felt her stomach flip flop from his declaration. She would never grow tired of hearing those three little words, as long as she lived. "I love you, too, Tobias Gable. What shall we ever do with the rest of our lives?" She turned to face him, smiling fondly.

Tobias leaned in closer, resting his forehead against hers. "We'll be extremly happy and serve Jesus with all of our hearts."

"Sounds like the perfect measure of happiness," she said, closing her eyes – reveling in the moment.

"Indeed it does," he replied. He thanked God for second chances and new beginnings. Their Heavenly Father had surely given them both one – a miracle amidst the mess – a love worth living for.

## Epilogue

It poured on their wedding day, great bucketfuls of rain. Many would have seen this as a bad omen, but Tilly and Tobias perceived it as God pouring his blessings down on them from Heaven.

"You're soaked to the bone, Wife," Tobias chuckled as Tilly squeezed out her drenched hair in front of the mirror.

Tilly smirked in disapproval. "So are you, Husband! Your hair is a sopping mess," she teased.

Tobias grinned. "I have a wedding gift for you, give me a

moment," he said, leaving the room they would spend their first night together as husband and wife. Butterflies fluttered madly in her abdomen with anticipation for what was to come. The Jacobs' had generously rented them a honeymoon suite at an upscale hotel for their wedding present. Tonight signaled the first night of the rest of their lives. When they returned home, they would settle down in her old farm house. Caleb and Trina had moved across town to a rent house which belonged to the Jacobs. Caleb had desired a place away from the farm. She knew it held many painful memories for them all, but Tilly had opted to stay and turn their house back into a home – her and Tobias's home. She wouldn't rip her sisters away from the only home they'd ever known. Nadine and Theresa would remain in her care until they reached adulthood. She couldn't imagine life without them, though she was grateful Lydia had bribed them to come and stay with her and Thomas for the summer, until she and Tobias could get settled into their new lives as a couple.

Tobias returned minutes later, cradling a small package in his hands. "Be careful, it's fragile," he added, transferring the gift into her awaiting hands. She nodded, opening it cautiously. She gasped when she saw what was inside – an alabaster box with two praying hands fastened to the lid.

"Oh, Tobias! It's so beautiful!" she gushed, lifting the lid to inspect the inside.

"I'm overjoyed you like it, I know it isn't like your mothers. Too bad we couldn't fix it," he remarked, shoving his hands in his suit pockets. She placed the box gently onto the bedside table, padding over to him in her stocking feet. Her white wedding gown hugged her svelte curves as she marched towards him, and he noticed, his eyes roaming over her, full of desire.

"It's perfect, Husband, I love it," she reassured him, cupping his face in her supple hands – kissing him breathlessly.

"You're so beautiful, angelic even," he muttered between kisses, shedding his suit jacket. Tilly giggled as he hoisted her over his shoulder, depositing her onto the bed. He tumbled after her, and she smiled happily as she wrapped her arms around him, kissing him again, which led to hundreds more as two souls became one.

With marriage, came children, and Tilly was astounded when God decided to give them twins – a boy and a girl. Tobias treated her with fragility during her pregnancy – caring for her around the clock. The fear of losing another child, including her, still resigned itself in the back of his mind. The day she gave birth was a harsh winter's day, but the twins both came out red and screaming – their lungs healthy and their appetites merciless.

When the twins were three, God called Tobias to pastor the church full time.  Reverend Vann was old and feeble.  He was grateful once Tobias agreed to take over.  The congregation's love for God grew as well as their numbers.  In their seventh year of marriage, the church was bursting at the seams, so they built a bigger and better one.

As the church grew, so did their family.  By the time Tilly's father was released from prison, the couple had five children.  Bart Matthews never drank another drop of liquor upon his release.  He spent his final years serving as an elder of the church – completely changed by the power of God's grace – and playing with his grandchildren.

As Nadine and Theresa grew older, Nadine developed a desire to work in the  healthcare industry and went off to college to become a nurse.  However, Theresa followed in her sister, Tilly's footsteps and became an artist.  Tilly corresponded with Starla Hennessee for years, encouraging her to take Theresa under her wing as her protégée.  The renowned artist had agreed, granting her the scholarship she'd once offered to Tilly.

As the years passed, Tilly never forgot her Mother's alabaster box or what she'd taught her. She filled her own with prayer requests. Blessed is she who has believed the Lord would fulfill his promises to her, is what Tilly lived by, for God had proved faithful through the ups and downs of her life.

**The End**

Made in the USA
Monee, IL
11 December 2019